Lena

Other books by Jacqueline Woodson:

Behind You

Locomotion

Hush

Miracle's Boys

If You Come Softly

The House You Pass on the Way

I Hadn't Meant to Tell You This

Between Madison and Palmetto

Maizon at Blue Hill

The Dear One

Last Summer With Maizon

Lena

by Jacqueline Woodson

G. P. Putnam's Sons

G. P. PUTNAM'S SONS
A division of Penguin Young Readers Group
Published by The Penguin Group
Penguin Group (USA) Inc., 375 Hudson Street, New York, NY 10014, U.S.A.
Penguin Group (Canada), 90 Eglinton Avenue East, Suite 700, Toronto, Ontario,
Canada M4P 2Y3 (a division of Pearson Penguin Canada Inc.).
Penguin Books Ltd, 80 Strand, London WC2R 0RL, England.
Penguin Ireland, 25 St. Stephen's Green, Dublin 2, Ireland (a division of Penguin Books Ltd.).
Penguin Group (Australia), 250 Camberwell Road, Camberwell, Victoria 3124, Australia
(a division of Pearson Australia Group Pty Ltd).
Penguin Books India Pvt Ltd, 11 Community Centre, Panchsheel Park, New Delhi - 110 017,
India.
Penguin Group (NZ), Cnr Airborne and Rosedale Roads, Albany, Auckland 1310, New Zealand
(a division of Pearson New Zealand Ltd).
Penguin Books (South Africa) (Pty) Ltd, 24 Sturdee Avenue, Rosebank,
Johannesburg 2196, South Africa.
Penguin Books Ltd, Registered Offices: 80 Strand, London WC2R 0RL, England.

Published simultaneously in Canada. Printed in the United States of America.
Published by arrangement with Random House Children's Books,
a division of Random House, Inc. First published in 1999 by Delacorte Press.
First G. P. Putnam's Sons Edition, 2006.
Design by Katrina Damkoehler. Text set in Berkeley Old Style.

Library of Congress Cataloging-in-Publication Data
Woodson, Jacqueline. Lena / Jacqueline Woodson.— 1st G.P. Putnam's Sons ed.   p. cm.
A sequel to: I hadn't meant to tell you this.
Summary: Thirteen-year-old Lena and her younger sister Dion mourn the death of their mother
as they hitchhike from Ohio to Kentucky while running away from their abusive father.
[1. Runaways—Fiction. 2. Sisters—Fiction.] I. Title.
PZ7.W868Le 2006   [Fic]—dc22   2005032666   ISBN 0-399-24469-7

1 3 5 7 9 10 8 6 4 2
First Impression

To brave girls everywhere

Lena

One

Mama died when I was nine. She used to all the time say to me that no matter what happened, I'd find myself on the other side of it. She'd say, "Don't you be scared none either, Lena, 'cause you got a right to be in the world just like everybody else walking through it." Then Mama would smile, pull my braid and set about to fixing dinner or cleaning up or, if we had a little extra money, she'd have some fabric that she'd cut into a dress for herself with matching ones for me and Dion. We hardly ever had extra money 'cause Daddy didn't work regular. Once in a while, he'd get work dynamiting coal. But by the time Mama started getting sick, most of the coal had been blown from the ground. We got by, though. We never had to beg anybody for anything and Mama made sure we ate regular.

Dion must of been about four when Mama died but she makes believe she doesn't remember a lick about her. Dion doesn't really understand about death so she just makes believe she never knew anybody that died. It's like she's got this box of Mama Memories locked up inside her head 'cause I know way deep down she has to remember how Mama used to hold her on her lap, how we'd all sit around that potbelly stove in the winter and Mama'd sing to us. She had a pretty voice, Mama did—all soft and high. We were living in Ripley then. West Virginia. Had us a tiny house down near Dunbar. West Virginia sky got all this blue in it, like sky you don't get to see in other places. Sometimes I'll get to drawing it, mixing different blues all up until I get it just so. Pictures I draw of West Virginia remind me of Mama, like maybe that's her inside of all that blue, looking down at us.

After that we lived in this apartment over Che Che's Beauty Care. That was in Ravenswood. Lived there for about a year until Che Che said she needed to be getting the rent on time and all at once, not in little bits and pieces. We went to Marietta, Ohio, from there.

Mama got sicker and sicker and finally died in Marietta. We had a little funeral for her in Champlain Field, a few miles outside of Marietta. I forgot the exact name of the town.

I don't remember crying much the day we buried Mama but I remember sort of listening to the preacher talk about ashes to ashes and the dearly departed. I was standing holding Dion's hand and my daddy was holding my other hand and there was a few old ladies, the kind that just sort of go from funeral to funeral the way normal people go to the movies.

For a long time, I'd forget Mama was dead and sit by the window waiting for her to come in from doing day work somewhere. After a while, I stopped sitting and the *knowing* settled down inside of me. Made itself a home there. A few years after Mama passed, we moved on up to Chauncey, Ohio. Me and Dion got ourselves settled in school there and for a while we seemed to be doing all right.

Sometimes when Dion gets to asking questions about Mama, I think maybe that's that locked box inside her head, opening up a bit. Some days we'll be walking and Dion'll look full at me and say something like "What color was Mama's eyes?" It's up to me to tell her everything she wants to know. Up to me to do all the remembering 'cause it's really only the two of us left now.

I should tell you I love my sister Dion more than anybody in the whole world. She's only eight now but I swear if you hear her talk sometimes you'd think she was a whole lot older. And when she gets mad, she starts to cursing like the devil. I don't know where she learned to curse like she do. I use my own curse words only every once in a while, not wasting them on something that don't need a good one thrown in there. Sometimes I think Dion must stay up late at night practicing to herself. And she's smart too. She reads real fast, always trying to sneak in a couple of pages of some book. Yesterday, we hitched a ride in a Laughing Cow Dairy truck with a Wisconsin plate—I wrote down the number. When you're hitching, you have to be careful about stuff like that, Dion says. In this short time she thinks she's some kind of pro. "You got the plate number?" she whispered to me, before we climbed in. I nodded. Thing is—you can take down all the plate numbers you want but if something bad happens to you, not much anybody can do about it. Especially for me and Dion. It's not like we got us some people somewhere just waiting to take care of business if something happened to us. But me and Dion figure, if anybody ever tried anything—we're gonna come back after them someday. Come back ourselves and fix that person. We don't need nobody. I got a half page of plate numbers. Right next to them, I write a little bit about each truck driver—you know, stuff like what they're hauling, how many kids they got, that kind of thing. My best friend, Marie, gave me this book before we left Chauncey. She said it was to draw in. But back in Chauncey, I got used to drawing on brown paper bags. I liked the way the colors seem quieter coming up off the brown. So I took to writing in this book instead. One day, maybe I'll see her again and I'll show Marie how much use I got out of it.

You know how sometimes you get to thinking about a person so hard, you start to hurt—not just inside your head or your stomach but all over the place? That's how it is when I get to thinking about Marie. My mind races back to that last night when me and Dion took off. Marie was at the other end of the phone begging me not to go. I still hear her voice inside my head. Marie's voice. My friend. I start thinking about real sad things when her voice comes on—about all the people who left her—like her mama who just took off one day and never came back. And me, just giving her a call and saying me and Dion had to go. But we *did* have to go. And there wasn't anything anybody in Chauncey could do. That's where my mind was yesterday when that Laughing Cow truck pulled over to the side of the road and a guy with a real nice smile said, "Get in."

I stood there a minute, eyeing the guy—my mind half on him, half on Marie. If a driver didn't look right, me and Dion'd just start walking. You could tell a lot about a person looking at their eyes. If a person's stone cold crazy, you can see it—their eyeballs twitch. I can tell crazy people from across the room so I don't have to walk right up to a truck to see it. Me and Dion say no to more rides than we say yeah to but it's gotta be that way if we want to make it where we going. I don't want to be one of those girls you read about.

It was cold out, gray, like maybe right behind us there was coming some rain or snow. I shook my head, trying to shake the Marie Memories out of it. The driver didn't look crazy—just tired. But I pushed Dion in ahead of me anyway. Truck drivers see somebody real young like Dion and they pretty much keep their hands to themselves. Most times, they got a kid Dion's age waiting at home for them.

Turned out the guy driving the Laughing Cow truck, Larry, had two kids at home and he just kept looking over at us, shaking his head like he couldn't believe we were out on the road this way. We probably look real young to a lot of people. I've heard people say I look old too—like some old lady that's seen too much of life. Marie used to say that. She'd say it was something about my eyes made me look older than thirteen. Me and her used to sit in Randolph Park and watch people. That's where I learned about the looks of crazy people, by watching while me and Marie talked.

"We really appreciate you stopping, sir," I said. "If it wasn't this kind of emergency, we wouldn't be traveling this way. It breaks my mama's heart that we don't have no people."

Larry shook his head and every now and then mumbled about what a shame it all was and how the world is more messed up than anybody would ever believe.

"You see things," Larry said. He had pretty eyes—blue with reddish lashes. When he talked he squinted them up, thinking. I made a note in my mind to write about Larry's eyes when he dropped us off. "When you're driving a truck all the time, you see things that would make your heart stand still."

"We saw dead deer on the road a couple of times," Dion said. She pulled a book out of the knapsack and started reading.

"Deers and kids and accidents," Larry said. "Whole families on the highway with their thumbs out . . ."

I listened to him go on a little bit while Dion sat there reading. I swear she read right on up till when it got dark. Then she put that book back in her knapsack and fell asleep. Larry was going on and on about how important families were and whatnot but I couldn't really listen anymore. To me, blood didn't mean anything. Only blood relative I had right out besides Dion was my daddy. I knew deep in his heart he was probably all kinds of good but on the surface, he was—he was messed up. Real messed up. After Mama died, he just started going downhill. I'd come home and he'd be sitting on the couch just staring at the wall. Then he'd see me and he'd smile. Only it was the smile he used to give Mama. Not a daddy-to-daughter smile. He wanted me to be Mama. But I'm not. I'm Lena.

I sat there listening to Larry but thinking about my daddy and wishing I was someplace alone where I could just cry and cry. Figure I get a good cry in somewhere, I wouldn't always be trying to swallow the tears back.

Dion sighed in her sleep. She's real pretty when she's sleeping—with her dark brown hair making her face look all soft. I had cut our hair real short before we left but even with it cut short, Dion still looked pretty—like a pretty boy. I watched the lights from oncoming cars move over her. She got Mama's pretty—Dion did. Me—I guess I look more like our daddy. My hair is just hair—brown and all full of cowlicks. Dion got Mama's bright blue eyes. My own eyes are kind of light brown—but just plain. I stared at Dion, wondering what's she gonna be like when she's grown, being so pretty and all. Wondering if people gonna always treat her like they do now—a little better than they treat regular-looking people.

"What your mama have herself?" Larry asked.

I blinked. I was staring so hard at Dion, I had forgotten he was there.

"Excuse me?" I stared straight ahead. From the first day, we knew not to look anybody right in the eyes. Seemed it was easier for people to tell you was lying when you looked at them.

"Your mama have a boy or a girl?"

"Girl." I looked at him out of the corner of my eye. He was grinning, like he was the proud daddy.

"My wife's working on a boy," he said. "I keep telling her next one'll be a girl just like the ones that came before her. Seems that's the way it works. You start having girls, you just keep on. Your mama want a boy?"

"She got two already. Me and my brother Dion here is probably a handful for her. Figure she was ready for a girl."

Larry looked at me but didn't say anything. The first night we got in a truck, this guy started trying to feel on me. He kept saying, "You such a pretty boy," and I had to keep slapping his hands away. I hoped I wouldn't have to be slapping at Larry's hands. I had figured us looking like boys would make hitching easier but some people didn't seem to care what you were. When we got into cars with ladies, we let ourselves be girls again 'cause seemed ladies wanted to be riding with girls. But with men truck drivers, me and Dion toughened up.

"Figure she just wanted a healthy baby, that's all. Me and Dion was born healthy and I hear this one was too."

Lying made my stomach hurt. We had told the same lie ever since Chauncey—that we were on our way to see our mama. That she'd just had a baby and had sent for us but somebody stole our money on the way. Dion had come up with the lie. We changed it a bit so we didn't get too bored with it, but mostly it stayed the same and I swear, every time somebody asked for details, my stomach got to aching.

I stared out at the dark highway and tried to switch my mind to something else. You on the road long enough, you get to thinking too deep about things. Some mornings, I'll be half-asleep and I'll start remembering all this stuff I don't want to be remembering, like the times I'd be sitting in the park with Marie worrying about Dion home alone with our daddy. How some days, I'd just take off in the middle of a conversation and run all the way home. And then I'd get home and Dion'd be there on her own sitting in front of the television with a bowl of cereal. I was always scared in Chauncey. Scared of my daddy. Scared of the mornings and the nights in our house. Scared for Dion. It was scary on the road but in a different way. It was easier to be afraid of strangers than to be afraid of your daddy. I put my arm around Dion's shoulder and pulled her closer to me. We were getting further and further away from Chauncey. Everything in my life was starting to feel like it happened a long time ago.

Larry had his brights on and every now and then a deer scooted along the bank. I felt like that deer, trying to get out of the way.

Every truck we climbed into was different. Larry's truck was filled with pictures of his family and smelled like the Jolly Rancher candies he kept scattered on the dash. The first truck we hitched smelled like fresh-killed chickens. The minute Dion stepped off, she started puking and made me swear I wouldn't make her ride in any more dead-animal trucks. Even though my stomach had been a little queasy that first day, I felt good. Good and free.

"Your daddy living?" Larry asked softly.

"No. He died of cancer."

Every single lie you tell just makes you remember the truth harder. Why couldn't that be the one thing that *wasn't* a lie? Why couldn't he have been the one to die instead of Mama? I turned back toward the window, hoping that was the end of it.

"Cancer took my daddy too. But that was a long time ago," he said quietly. "Shoot, I wasn't much older than you." He tapped a finger against the pictures on the dash. "That's why I'm going to be a good daddy to my girls," he said. "I ain't gonna leave them standing."

I looked over at him. Larry turned to me then looked away real quick. "I don't mean to say your daddy was a bad man."

"I figure you don't."

He cleared his throat. "We get to Owensboro I'ma give you and your little brother some money to get yourselves—"

"We'll be fine once—"

Larry held up his hand. "I know you're proud. I could look at you and tell that. But you just gonna have to swallow it for a bit. No telling what could go wrong between now and the next minute and when I let you and your brother off in front of that hospital tomorrow morning—I want to feel all right about it. Now if you feeling real bad about it, you can take one of my cards off that dashboard and mail the money right back to me when you-all in a safe place."

I reached onto the dashboard and took a card from a stack held together with a rubber band. It was too dark to read it so I stuck it in Dion's knapsack.

"Thank you, sir. I'm sure our mama will get it right back in the mail to you."

"That's fine. Just so long as it goes from my hand to yours."

Larry looked over at me again. After a moment, he smiled. It was a sad smile.

"You tell your mama she's doing a fine job, you hear. You tell her she's raising two good boys."

I nodded, feeling my own smile coming on. I was doing a fine job raising us. A fine job.

Two

It was near daylight when Larry pulled into one of those all-night diners just outside of Owensboro, Kentucky. "You-all wait here," he said. "I'll get directions to the hospital." He disappeared inside and I rolled down my window and took a look around. Owensboro looked bigger than a lot of other towns we'd been through. We'd passed lots of tobacco fields and what looked to be factories. I stared out at the silos and barns, near-black in the half–light of daytime, and at the remains of cornfields picked clean as skeletons. Then I sighed and leaned back against the seat.

Larry came out carrying a brown paper bag. "Brought y'all some sandwiches," he whispered, climbing up into the truck and handing me the bag. "Ham and cheese. Y'all do eat ham, don't you?"

I nodded. "Thank you."

"Thank you," Dion mumbled.

Larry smiled and started the truck up again. "Seems everybody's not eating something these days—no meat, no dairy, no wheat. Seems like somebody's just trying to keep farmers out of work, that's all. Hospital's only four miles down the road. Lady in there said you can't miss it."

Dion fell asleep again as we drove, her breath soft against my shoulder.

When Larry tried to pull his rig up to the hospital, a guard told him he'd have to park at the Trailways station across the street. Larry frowned as he backed up.

"See what I mean about anything could happen?"

I nodded. Dion woke up and looked around, all sleepy-eyed.

"We here already?"

Larry pulled to a stop. I climbed down from the truck and kicked my legs out a bit. Dion climbed down and did the same thing.

"You take this," he said, getting out of the truck and pressing some bills in my hand. He took a look around the station. "I gotta get moving but you kids take care of yourselves."

He gave us a look. "Don't talk to no strangers."

"We won't," me and Dion said at the same time.

Then Larry was climbing back into his truck and backing it out of the Trailways station. One day I'd get me a truck. Eat up a whole lot of road.

"He was nice."

"Yeah," Dion said. "I wish I was his kid. Wish I was going home to his house."

"No you don't. You wouldn't be with me then. You want to be with me, don't you?"

Dion looked away from me and nodded. "I have to pee," she said, and went on inside the station.

I took my knapsack off my shoulder and hunkered down on it. There wasn't a soul around and from the way the sky looked, all pink and new, I figured it wasn't even six o'clock in the morning.

"It's gonna be a pretty day," I said softly when Dion came out a few minutes later. I rubbed my eyes, hard, making believe there was something in them. I missed Chauncey, missed going to Marie's house on Saturday mornings. Her house was always clean and warm and there was always lots of good stuff to eat like somebody had just gone food shopping the day before. I wanted to pick up a pay phone and call, say, *Hey, Marie, I'm sorry I left in such a hurry. Wasn't nothing you did, you know.* But I couldn't. What if my daddy had police tapping the phones in Chauncey? What if Marie's own daddy answered and took to asking me a million questions to find out where we were? Or even worse, what if Marie told him about my daddy and the foster care people were searching for us the way they did a long time ago—waiting to catch us and send Dion one place and me another? Foster care people don't care about separating us. I rubbed my eyes harder, feeling the tears pushing through. No matter what, me and Dion had to stay together.

"You crying, Lena?" I felt Dion's little hand on my shoulder.

"What would I be crying for?" I gave my eyes one more wipe and glared at her.

Dion shrugged. She took a step back from me, hunkered down on her own knapsack. We must of been a sight—two kids in flannel shirts and jeans and hiking boots at a Trailways station—Dion chewing on her collar, me with my head in my hands.

"Lena?"

She swallowed, like she was a little bit scared of what she was gonna say.

"Where we going, Lena? You tell me that and I won't ask you anything else—ever again if you don't want me to."

People on the outside who didn't understand would probably look at me and Dion and say, "Those kids are running away from home." But I knew we was running *to* something. And to someplace far away from Daddy. Someplace safe. That's where we were going.

"Mama's house," I whispered, my voice coming out hoarse and shaky. "We going to Mama's house."

Dion shook her head. "Not the lies we tell people—the true thing. Where we going for real?"

"Mama's house," I said again, looking away from her.

"Lena?" Dion said. "Mama's . . . *dead.*"

I swallowed. Dion hadn't used that word for Mama before. It sounded strange coming out of her mouth. Wrong somehow. I squinted at some cars, then up at the sky where the pink was starting to fade into blue. Beautiful days broke me up inside. They made me think of all the kids in the world who could just wake up in the morning and pull the curtain back from their windows and stare out at the day and smile. I wanted that kind of life for Dion. I was too old to be wishing that for myself.

"I know she's dead. I didn't say we was going to her. I said we was going to her house."

"And what's gonna happen when we get there?"

"You said you wasn't gonna ask no more questions, Dion."

Dion nodded and pulled her book out of her knapsack. I took a box of colored pencils out of mine and the brown paper bag our sandwiches had come in and started sketching. I sketched the field across the way from us and a blue car moving in front of it. I sketched the sky with the pink still in it and Dion sitting on her knapsack reading. Maybe we sat there an hour. Maybe two or three. We'd learned how to make ourselves invisible. Most people didn't take a second look if they saw us—two boys sitting doing nothing. Sometimes we hung out at libraries. Dion loved those days 'cause she got to just read and read. And some days we went to a park if it was nice. But mostly we sat in hospital waiting rooms. Before I left Chauncey, I'd gone to the library and looked up all the hospitals I could find in Kentucky, West Virginia and Ohio. People were always rushing around hospitals, thinking about their sick and their dying. They didn't have time to stop and notice us sitting there—or if they did, I guess they figured we were waiting for some grown-up who was visiting. I'd usually let Dion sleep while I kept a lookout. If we found a car unlocked, it was good for sleeping in at night, but most times we slept in the woods. I'd learned to sleep real light and listen out.

I put a nurse in my drawing, then an old lady in a wheelchair. Soon a bus pulled in. Then another one. Some people got off. Some people got on. Me and Dion watched them. There was a skinny girl around Dion's age carrying a suitcase. Dion narrowed her eyes at the girl, then went back to reading her book.

"How much money we got?"

Dion didn't even look up from her book. "About ninety-eight dollars."

When we left Chauncey, turned out Dion had seventy-two dollars stashed in this old yellow sock she had stuck way back in her drawer. That's how smart she is—only eight and was already saving for some rainy day. All along, I'd been trying to save everything I could too. Some days, I'd go down to the Winn-Dixie and pack up groceries for people. After buying us knapsacks and some supplies, I had about thirty dollars left.

I counted the bills from Larry. "Another forty here. You hungry?"

"A little. We could eat the sandwiches he bought us."

"That's lunch food. Lunch food's for lunch."

"A person can eat a ham and egg sandwich for breakfast," Dion said. "Why can't they eat a ham and cheese sandwich?"

"It's got mayo and lettuce on it, that's why. Mayo and lettuce ain't for breakfast. Mess your day all up eating the wrong thing at the wrong time. Just 'cause we kind of in between homes now don't mean we start acting like we don't have home-training."

I got up off my knapsack and looked around the station. "I bet you there's a town to this place with a little diner or something where we could get us some breakfast food."

Dion tore her eyes away from her book and squinted up at me. She didn't look scared like a lot of little kids. Just small and—I don't know—like she trusted me.

"Let's head over that way and get us a ride." I pointed out toward the fields. "Seems more cars heading left than right so we should hitch left."

"They going west," Dion said, putting her knapsack on her shoulders and stuffing that book in her back pocket. She's smarter than me about things like east and west. Numbers too. And she knows a lot of big words. If you're reading a book and you come across a word you don't know, she could probably tell you what it means, save you a trip to the dictionary. Lot of people'd be embarrassed if their kid sister was smarter than them but I figure me and Dion more of a team than other people. She fixes my words and numbers and I save her from our daddy. I keep it so she can read in peace and not be scared to go to sleep at night.

"What you reading anyway?"

"Just some poems."

"They rhyme?"

Dion shook her head. "I don't like the rhyming kind anymore. Those are for babies."

"You gonna read me one later?"

"If you want me to, I guess." She slipped her little skinny arm around my waist and we started walking.

"It's gonna get cold again soon," she said, looking up at the sky. "It's too warm for December."

"I know." But I didn't want to think about it. It was December but for some reason it was warm again, like spring some days. At night it got real cold but in the daytime, I swear the temperature would climb to sixty degrees. I swallowed, remembering Chauncey, how right before it snowed there had been this Indian summer and me and Marie had walked around with our coats hanging from our heads. Besides our rain jackets, me and Dion only had flannel shirts and heavy sweaters now. It had been so warm when we left Chauncey, we left our coats behind because we didn't want to look suspicious. Every day I held my breath, hoping this wouldn't be the day it got real cold out.

"They call it the greenhouse effect," Dion was saying. "It's 'cause of chemicals or something."

"What's 'cause of chemicals?"

"The *warm*," Dion said, sounding annoyed. "I bet you every year it's going to get hotter and hotter and soon the earth's gonna just catch on fire. Boom! The end."

I looked at her and smiled. "You read too much."

"Wait and see. When you know December to be warm like this?"

We got to the road and I stuck out my thumb. "We're just lucky, Dion. Got weather on our side."

"Got *chemicals* on our side. Cop car coming."

I put my thumb down fast and me and Dion started walking again, my heart beating hard against my chest.

The cop car pulled up alongside of us and slowed down.

"Where you two headed so early in the morning?" The cop tried to smile but it was a small smile.

I looked him straight in the eye and tried to keep my voice steady. "School, sir."

"Well, school's in the other direction, isn't it? You two taking the long way."

"Figure we'd get some breakfast first. Our mama went into labor last night and our daddy still with her at the hospital. We don't know how to cook yet." I held out my hand and showed him a ten-dollar bill. "Mama left this money in case of emergency. Breakfast is kind of an emergency."

The cop frowned down into my hand like he was trying to figure out what a ten-dollar bill was. Then he gave me and Dion another hard look.

"You two headed over to Berta's?"

"Berta's . . . diner?"

"What other Berta's is there?"

"Yes sir," Dion said real quick, then ducked her head again.

"Well then, get in the back. And use your change to take a car service back to school. No use you boys being late on account of a baby coming."

$\mathcal{B}$erta's was at the end of a dusty-looking strip of stores. There was a Piggly Wiggly, a Coleen's Beauty Parlor and a dance school that looked abandoned. I stared at the dingy pink ballet slippers painted across the front window. I used to want to be a dancer when I was real little. Mama'd always said the minute her ship came in she'd pay for me to take some lessons. I'm a good dancer when I set my mind to it. Once, me and Marie put bottle caps on our sneakers and danced out in front of the drugstore. Some people stopped and watched us and that made me feel real good. This old man handed us each a dollar. Me and Marie sure laughed hard about that one.

"Come on, Lena," Dion said, pulling my hand. "Before that cop gets to sniffing around us again."

I followed her inside the diner. It was quiet and warm. A couple of old men were sitting along the counter drinking coffee. We took a seat at one of the booths.

"Can I get pancakes?"

I nodded. "You better get some bacon or sausage or something. Fill yourself up so we can hold on to those sandwiches awhile. Don't know where we'll be come nighttime."

Dion looked at me real quick but didn't say anything.

The waitress came up to our table. She was pretty, with curly hair and a nose ring. Didn't look much older than me.

"What can I get you early birds?" she said.

"A menu, please," Dion said, sounding like she ate at restaurants all the time.

The waitress smiled, then disappeared and came back with two menus. We ordered the Breakfast Special—pancakes, sausage, two eggs, home fries and toast.

"You two kind of hungry this morning, huh?"

I nodded. "And orange juice too, please—for both of us."

After she left, I pulled our toothbrushes out of my knapsack. Our tube of toothpaste was almost flat. "Here, Dion, you go wash up first." I handed her her toothbrush underneath the table, all the while looking around to make sure nobody was watching. "Run your fingers through your hair and make sure you throw some water on your face."

There was one of those tiny jukeboxes on the wall beside our table. After Dion left, I flipped through it, looking at all the songs. There was mostly country with one or two songs that if I wanted to waste the dollar, I'd actually consider playing. When I got to the end, I started flipping through it again. I was trying hard not to think about where we'd be come nighttime.

Dion used to be afraid about the night. A lot of trucks had these little beds in the back and if a truck driver was real nice, they'd tell us to climb back there for a couple of hours. Once, we hitched with this lady truck driver. She had the most comfortable bed I'd ever slept in.

I sat back in the booth and let my breath out real slow. With all the hitching and sleeping we'd done over the weeks, we could well be in California by now. But we were mainly traveling zigzag, trying to stay close to towns rather than getting way out there on the highway. We hitched in cars more than in trucks 'cause with cars you usually got a nice family type person. I frowned and flipped through the jukebox another time. I didn't know where we'd sleep tonight.

When Dion slipped back in the booth, I took the toothpaste from her and stuffed it in my pocket beside my own toothbrush. Dion took her book out and started reading again.

In the bathroom, I peed, then gave myself a good long hard look. My cheekbones seemed to be sticking out more than usual. My whole face looked different—older somehow. All the parts of my face together don't add up to much but separate, if I wasn't frowning, they looked fine. My shoulders made me look skinnier than I actually was, more like a boy than a girl, especially with my hair cut short. I took my flannel shirt off and tied it around my waist. Underneath, me and Dion were both wearing navy blue thermal shirts with T-shirts under them because Dion had read somewhere that layers are the best way to go if you're traveling. After I brushed my teeth and threw some warm water on my face, I checked in the mirror again. I was doing a fine job. But I needed to get us somewhere before the cold settled in.

When I got back to the table, the waitress was setting down tall glasses of orange juice. She gave me a long look, then pulled her lips to the side of her mouth.

"You two on the road?"

I swallowed, looking away from her. As long as we kept ourselves halfway clean, most people couldn't tell anything about us. But this waitress knew a whole lot of things. I could tell by the way she looked at me. Some people could look right through you and see everything you buried inside yourself.

"Yeah," Dion said quickly. "We're on the road to see our mama at Owensboro Hospital. She just had herself a baby boy."

The waitress gave us another long look and I could tell she didn't believe Dion.

"Yeah," she said. "I was on the road to see my daddy. He'd had surgery. And my friend Hadley was going to see her sick grandma." She smiled.

"It's the truth," Dion whispered, her eyes narrowing.

"I know," the waitress said. "It's always the truth, isn't it? How old are y'all anyway? Look to me about nine and eleven."

"I won't see nine again," Dion said. "Until it's a hundred and nine. And my brother probably old as you."

The waitress smiled. I could tell she liked Dion. "A mouth like that'll get you anywhere you want to go. Thing about being on the road is, people who figure out your secret are the ones you can trust. Those people probably got a closet full of skeletons same as yours. The ones who can't figure it out are the ones you worry about."

Dion didn't say anything.

"How long you been on your way?"

We didn't say anything. Dion took a long drink of orange juice and glared at the waitress.

"You keeping to back roads, staying away from truckers?"

I looked down at my hands. "Yeah."

"Look," the waitress whispered. "I wouldn't turn y'all in if somebody paid me. It's not like that. I was on the road a long time and I learned some things. You two might be fooling a lot of people trying to look like boys but I had the same costume so I know. You look young, so stay near young-looking places—schools and libraries and such. Don't stay any one place too long either. Keep moving."

"We're going to see our mama," Dion said. "She . . . had . . . herself . . . a . . . baby . . . boy! It's called plain English."

The waitress smiled and shook her head. "Well then, you send your mama my best," she said. "And I'll be back in a bit with your breakfasts, which are on me. You-all keep your money. Be needing it."

After she left, Dion glared at me. "You better learn how

to hold on to your lies, Lee," she said through her teeth. "I don't care if you don't know where the hell we're going or what's gonna happen when we get there. I ain't about to spend time in anybody's orphan house or jail."

"She's not gonna tell nobody, Dion. You heard her. She been on the road same like us. And look at her. She made it to the other side. Got herself a job and everything."

I turned the saltshaker around and around in my hand, trying not to smile. It felt good to have someone know. Somebody who'd taken the same trip and ended up in a small diner in a little town—all right.

Three

Maybe twice in my life I've broken somebody's heart. The night we left Chauncey, I broke Marie's. I guess next to Dion, Marie's the person I love most in the world. Before Marie came along, I hadn't had me a best friend in a long time. Seemed with all our moving and all, it just didn't happen. When we lived over Che Che's I had me a friend. We was real tight for a while but then Daddy said he didn't care much for me hanging around black people. We moved soon after that. Then I just had me, Dion and Mama but nobody on the outside.

Back in Chauncey, there wasn't a whole lot of white people and the black people who lived there, well, most of them didn't care too much for white people. The white people living there were like my daddy—he don't like black people and he'll say it right out. I don't know what's worse—not liking somebody because of their race or saying it right out. Both things tear a person up inside. At Chauncey Middle School, black kids sat on one side of the cafeteria, the white kids sat on the other. Same in the classroom—you'd see the two or three white kids all huddled together. My daddy used to always say united we stand, divided we fall, and I truly think all the kids at Chauncey had daddies at home saying the same thing.

Marie had this group of black girls she hung with. They were voted Most Popular and Best Dressed and all. They just floated through the school—white kids and black kids stepping out of their way.

When I first got to the Chauncey school, my teacher, Ms. Cory, made Marie show me around. You could tell Marie didn't like me, the way her face was all frowned up whenever she had to take me to a classroom or something. Anyway, this one day, we was in the bathroom. Marie was kind of crying 'cause her friends had been making fun of her and when I came in, she was washing her face, trying to make believe she wasn't crying. Thing about Marie, sometimes, when it was just the two of us, she'd get sweet. I knew that sweet side was her true self so it made me feel real bad to see her crying.

Marie's daddy was a professor at the university and since she was the only child, he bought her anything she wanted. Sometimes I'd see her sitting in a classroom dressed nice with her hair done up and I'd wish it was me that had all those nice things. Then Marie would look up at me and smile and I'd feel bad for being jealous. Her mama left them and it was just Marie and her dad so she deserved every single nice thing she had. Her mama hadn't even told her where she went—just sent these post-cards from all over the place with no return address on them. I guess her mama was the first one in the world to break her heart, then I came along and broke it again.

I think the main reason we became friends is 'cause we didn't have mamas. We used to talk about all kinds of things but mostly about what it was like not to have one.

That day in the bathroom, we still weren't friends yet but we got to talking and I asked her about her father. I always want to know about other people's daddies 'cause my own was so messed up. Marie told me a little bit about her daddy, that he didn't really like white people and all. I told Marie that my own daddy didn't like black people— that he was always calling them the *n* word—and her face sort of fell apart. That word is like a punch—every time I hear it I think about the way Marie's face looked when I said it. I would never say that word again. Anyway, we kind of started to become friends after that. Marie had this way of laughing that would make her whole face light up. And when you talked to her, she'd look right at you like what you had to say was the most interesting thing in the world. Some people, when you talk to them, they start looking in a hundred and two different directions, even at their watches like they can't wait for you to shut up and listen to them. Marie wasn't like that.

I think I'd rather have my heart broke than do the breaking. When you break somebody's heart you don't only have their sadness to carry around but you got your own guilty feelings too. That night I called Marie to tell her me and Dion was leaving, she cried and told me not to go. *We could tell somebody. Please don't go.* And you know something? If Dion wasn't standing beside me with her knapsack, if I hadn't already left that house and made up my mind to get us as far away from my daddy as I could, if I didn't feel like I would fly apart if I didn't leave when I did, then maybe I would have stayed.

Four

You ever want to see something sad you take a good look at a crying kid running toward somebody. You see all this hurt and scared in their faces. The night we left, Dion ran out of the house after me saying, "Don't go without taking me, Lena. I know you ain't coming back."

I didn't have the first desire to leave without Dion. She was the whole reason I was getting us out of there. When Mama died and Daddy got to touching on me, I started making plans. But those were stupid and didn't work out like I wanted them to. Now I had another plan. And this one would work, sure as I was born.

Every morning, I'd go out behind the house and check on the supplies I kept hidden beneath somebody's junked car. It seemed like forever I had been putting stuff together—an old tarp I'd found by a campsite, a water bottle I'd taken from Winn-Dixie, socks and long underwear, sweaters, me and Dion's blue plastic rain slickers, a flashlight, high-energy bars and blankets. I needed us to be ready for any kind of weather. Ready for anything. I'd had my number of nights sleeping outside and I knew how cold could settle right down into your bones and kill you if you weren't careful. Some nights I'd just go out there and pack and unpack the stuff to make sure it fit good in the knapsacks. We couldn't take a whole lot of stuff 'cause I wanted us to look like two kids on their way to school. I'd learned how to roll the blankets up real tight, make them the size of a sweater.

I was out behind the house packing up our stuff for the last time the night Dion came running toward me. I had just come from riding around with our daddy trying to talk to him, trying to convince him that it wasn't right him touching on Dion. But he'd just made believe I was crazy, that he wasn't doing anything out of place. It was bad enough my daddy was touching me but touching Dion was another story. I was already too old to have big dreams of being somebody but Dion was just a little kid.

When I turned around and saw Dion, I shoved the stuff back under the car real fast and leaned against it, scared.

"You can't leave without me, Lena," Dion said, wiping

her nose with the back of her hand. What if Dion froze to death? People would say it would have been better to keep her with our daddy than having her freeze. Me, if I froze, even that would be better than living the way we lived. But maybe not for Dion. I mean, what if she didn't have the strength to be on the road?

"What makes you think I'm going someplace, girl?"

Dion nodded toward the car. "All this time you've been packing stuff under that car. You even packed my little blue pillow—the one somebody sewed for me."

"Mama sewed that pillow for you."

Dion stared at me without saying anything.

I looked at the ground, remembering something I had tried to forget. Right after Mama died, this woman came from the child welfare department. When I told her about our daddy making me sleep in the same bed with him, she took me and Dion away. Then she sent Dion one way and me the other. It was the first time we'd ever been separated. And it was gonna be the last time too.

"You remember when you was still in Nelsonville and they'd sent me down near Kentucky?"

Dion nodded and wiped her eyes with the back of her hand.

"You remember how I ran away and come to get you and then we found our daddy again?"

"Yeah."

"Remember how cold it was?"

Dion shook her head. "No. I don't remember being cold."

"You remember being scared?"

"Uh-uh," Dion said. "You just came and got me and then we found him and then it was the three of us together again."

"It took us four days to get back to him. It was cold and you was scared, Dion!" I swallowed, wanting her to remember, remember and be ready. "You was *real* cold and *real* scared."

Dion glared at me. "Maybe it was you the one scared. Like you scared now."

"I ain't scared," I said quietly.

I frowned and looked up at the sky. It was almost nightfall. Somebody was playing music in one of the houses near ours, a country song about a man loving his woman forever and ever amen. Dion wrapped her arms around herself and watched me.

"You know he made me drive with him to town tonight?" I started chewing on my pinky finger. Somebody's dog was barking.

When I looked at Dion, her eyes seemed to disappear, like the whole inside of her was taking off somewhere.

"Later he's gonna call to you, you know. The way he does some nights."

Dion shrugged but her bottom lip was starting to tremble. She was wearing an old pair of summer pajamas and two buttons were missing on the top. She held it closed with one hand and wiped her eyes with the other. I took my jacket off and put it around her shoulders.

"It's not like this with everybody, Dion. It don't have to be this way with us. But it'll mean never seeing him again."

"Never?" Dion whispered.

I shook my head. Dion loved our daddy in a way I didn't anymore.

"Not for birthdays or nothing."

"Like if he's dead, Lena?" Dion asked.

"Yeah. Like that." I felt my heart getting tight in my chest. "You coming?"

Dion pulled my jacket tighter around her shoulders, her eyes getting teary.

I closed my eyes, hoping to hear Dion say no. If she said no, it would mean I tried and that she'd made a decision to stay here. If she said no, I'd have to stay 'cause I couldn't leave her. Maybe this wasn't as bad as the road. Maybe—

"I'm going with you, Lena."

I opened my eyes and smiled, the fear draining out of me. Me and Dion, we needed each other.

"He's gonna be back home around eight. We need to be gone before he gets here. First thing you gotta do is go get the scissors so I can cut our hair."

Dion's hand flew up to her ponytail. It wasn't a long one but she was pretty proud of it. "I'm not cutting my hair off."

"*I'm* cutting our hair off," I said. "We need people to think we're boys. It's safer that way."

Dion frowned, still holding on to her ponytail. I ran my fingers through my own hair. It wasn't that long 'cause I'd just cut it a few months back. But it needed to be shorter than it was.

"People think we boys, they'll leave us alone. You coming with me or not?"

Dion didn't say anything, just turned toward the house. I stood there with my arms folded, my heart beating fast again.

After a moment, Dion came back out carrying the scissors far away from her like they were disgusting. She had wet her head down and water was dripping onto my jacket. She handed me the scissors and turned around. We didn't say anything as I clipped and the hair landed in chunks around our feet.

"Don't make me look like a fool," she said. "Make it have a little style to it."

"Girl, I know what I'm doing." I pulled her ear down and cut the hair above it in a straight line. Her hair didn't have the slightest bit of curl to it.

"People ask," I said. "Your name is Ed. Be easy 'cause it's short for Edion."

"How come they can't just call me Dion—that's almost a boy's name."

"'Cause Ed's better."

"Well, I like Dion."

I rolled my eyes. It wasn't worth fighting over. "Okay, then Dion. My name's Lee, though. Say it."

"Lee," Dion said softly. "Ain't like it's the hardest thing to remember."

"Just remember we boys, okay? Don't slip up and go into the ladies' bathroom by accident—"

"I ain't using no men's room! You crazy?"

"What'll happen if somebody says 'young man—that's the ladies' room.'"

"Then I'll tell them I ain't a young man. I could get snatched right up in the men's room!"

I thought about this for a moment. It was true—we didn't need to be taking no chances going into the men's bathroom.

"Okay," I said. "If we have to hitchhike with men, then we say we boys. Everyplace else we can be girls. But try to be a boy as much as possible."

Dion nodded. I finished cutting her hair and turned her this way and that. From the right angle, she looked like a soft little boy.

"Clean up all that hair and throw it away," I said.

"You don't want me to cut yours?"

"No. I'll do it." I took the scissors into the bathroom and stared at myself in the mirror for a moment. My face was pale and drawn like Mama's was when she was sick. I stuck my head under the faucet to wet my hair, then started cutting. After a moment, Dion came in and looked at herself in the mirror. She reached back where her ponytail used to be and our eyes met. It was real. Her hair was gone and we were leaving.

"It's just hair," she said. She ran her fingers through it, looked at me again and left me to my business.

I didn't waste a whole lot of time. When I was finished, my hair was shorter than it'd ever been. I narrowed my eyes and sneered, trying to look tough, like a boy.

Dion came back in while I was flushing the hair down the toilet.

"It looks nice."

"You like yours?" I asked.

Dion shrugged. "When we get to where we going, I'm gonna grow it all the way down my back."

I swallowed, not wanting to think about where we were going right yet.

"We got to get moving," I said. "He'll be home soon and we got to be on our way."

Dion followed me back outside without saying anything. I pulled the stuff out from beneath the car. If I didn't want us to spend one more night in the same house with him, I couldn't be scared. Not for Dion. Not for me. Not for anybody.

"He'll be worrying for us, Lena."

I made out like I didn't hear her. "We'll be sleeping in boxes in dark alleys. Probably have to spend a night in a garbage can or two." I pulled Dion's blue pillow out and gave it to her.

"Box'll keep the wind away," she said softly, pressing her head into the pillow.

"Won't be no hot chocolate and warm baths like we get at Marie's house, Dion."

"You gone, I reckon I wouldn't spend much time with Marie anyways. Seeing as she's really your friend and all. And wasn't no warm baths last time we were on the road."

"I thought you didn't remember."

"Said I didn't remember being cold and scared. That's all."

"Go inside and get those wool socks I bought us—and some books you want but not a whole lot. Put on your boots and a pair of thick socks, two pairs—and a T-shirt under your clothes."

"Layers keep us warmer than just regular clothes."

"Then put two T-shirts on, girl—and something warm. Go!"

Dion turned and ran back into the house. I looked through the pile, trying to decide if there was anything we wouldn't need. We were gonna be free soon. Free.

Dion came back outside and threw me the socks, then ran back in again.

I rolled the tarp up and stuffed it inside a pillowcase, then set about getting everything into some kind of order. It was dark out but not too cold. I pulled my sleeve back and looked at my watch. A long time ago it had belonged to Mama. It was near to seven-thirty.

I stuffed a bunch of things into my knapsack. There was a pile of paperback books I'd already put in the bottom of Dion's. I started to take some out, then stopped and just put as much as I could on top of them. I wiped my hand across my forehead and was surprised to see that I was sweating.

Dion came back out carrying some more books and trying to pull on her boot at the same time.

"Girl, you trying to take the whole shelf?"

"I can fit a few in my pockets," she said.

I took the books from her and stuffed some of them into my pack. The rest I took back inside. Then I took a quick check around the house, making sure we'd left things in a way that he wouldn't come looking for us right away. In the bathroom, I pulled on my blue ski cap, then lifted my shirt and wrapped an Ace bandage tight around my chest. I didn't have too much to make me look like a girl but the little bit I had, I wanted to hide. Dion didn't have to worry.

When I came back outside, Dion was putting the last of her books into her knapsack.

"I got a book of maps in my pocket," she said, eyeing me. "You figure we need them?"

"Kentucky in there?"

"Uh-huh. Is that where we going? What's in Kentucky, Lena?"

"If Kentucky's in there," I said, ignoring her questions, "then pack it."

"That's where we going, Lena?" she asked again. "Kentucky?"

"You better get to tying your boot instead of asking so many questions or else the *you* part of this *we* ain't going nowhere." I knew I was lying but it made her move faster.

"Where's my hat? How come you get one and I don't?"

I threw her an orange cap and lifted the knapsack on my shoulders. She put the cap on and looked at me. "Get that bag on your shoulders and let's go."

That night, after I called Marie from a pay phone, me and Dion walked right on out of Chauncey. A lady in a blue car with Ohio plates drove us as far as Athens. We found woods to sleep in there.

I didn't look back that night. Didn't want to see Chauncey disappearing behind me. Getting smaller and smaller until it became another place and another time.

Five

It got real cold the night after we arrived in Owensboro. Me and Dion slept bundled up in our sweaters behind the Winn-Dixie. Some nights I prayed someone would come pick us up, take us someplace warm. But I knew in my heart I didn't want to go to some police station or shelter to sleep in a room full of strangers, wake up to some social worker lady prying into our business.

The next morning, me and Dion went to the Salvation Army to get coats. Dion found herself this big old peacoat. It looked real cute on her with her scraggly hair. I told her she looked just like one of the Beatles—that band from the old days. Dion started dancing around the store, singing some crazy song about Strawberry Fields. A lot of kids wouldn't know who the Beatles were, but Dion even knew one of their songs.

I got me a red bomber jacket with a hood that had fake fur around the edge. It kept my ears good and warm. The pockets had holes so I couldn't even think about putting something in them, but if I jammed my hands in and balled them up into fists, they stayed warm. I pulled Dion's collar up over her ears. The calendar next to the cash register said Saturday, December 29.

"Is that the right date?" I asked the lady who rang up our coats.

She looked at me kind of funny and nodded.

"Thank you." I took the change she handed me and we headed out.

"Be two weeks tomorrow," Dion said softly.

"I know. Don't seem that long, does it?"

Dion shook her head. "Seems longer. We missed Christmas."

"We knew it was coming." Every town we ended up in had Christmas decorations up in store windows and on the lampposts. It was hard to not see it. Even the air smelled like Christmas—all piney and cold.

"Yeah," Dion said. "But we didn't know it came."

I tried to think where we had been on Christmas Day— maybe Marietta or somewhere. A lot of stores had been closed one day and maybe that was Christmas.

We crossed the street and sat down on a bench at a bus stop.

"When we was little, Mama used to always make us a ham on Christmas and sweet potatoes and corn bread—a whole lot of food. But the only thing you'd eat was the corn bread. Mama used to say she'd never seen a baby eat as much corn bread as you."

Dion smiled and I kept talking.

"She used to always wear her hair in this French braid that hung down her back and on Christmas, she'd do me and your hair up the same way and we'd just sit in front of the mirror looking at ourselves and eating candy canes. Even if we didn't have a tree, we always had candy canes. And Mama always looked so happy on Christmas morning. She was tall and pretty and, before she got sick, she used to always laugh. Me and you could always make her laugh. And then she'd hug us and ask, 'Who's your favorite mama?'"

"And what would we answer?" Dion asked, even though I'd told her this story a hundred times.

I smiled and grabbed her. Dion laughed. "The one who can hug us the tightest!" I gave Dion a tight hug and smiled.

"And that's what she'd do," I said.

"I got a frog once," Dion said. "A stuffed frog, right?"

"You loved that frog from the minute Mama gave it to you. You slept with it all the time."

"What happened to it?"

I took my hands out of my pockets and blew on them. Dion shivered and moved closer to me.

"Huh, Lee? Where'd that frog go?"

I frowned. Every time we moved, something got lost. It was like there were these parts of us scattered all over the place. "I guess you got tired of it after a while."

"Oh," Dion said, but I knew she didn't believe me.

"When we grow up, Dion, let's always have a big Christmas with lots of food and presents and music."

"And a grand piano we can stand around and sing songs. And it'll always snow on Christmas morning, right?"

I nodded. "Always—big white flakes just slowly coming down like they got all the time in the world."

Across the street, a group of little kids were walking in a line. Dion's eyes flicked over to them, then away again real fast. She got quiet.

"You okay, girlie?" I reached over and rubbed my hand across her head.

"And hot chocolate with whip cream," she said softly.

"Yeah. In big white mugs that we have to hold with both hands."

Dion didn't say anything, just kind of narrowed her eyes at the kids. I knew the dreaming was over for now. We got up and started walking again, Dion with her head hanging down.

"You missing school, right? I know how much you like it."

She looked at me and shrugged. The wind was whipping around us like it had lost its mind. Dion's teeth were chattering so I pulled her close to me. Soon as we got settled somewhere, I'd figure out a way to sign her up.

"I figure we could go get us some hot chocolate and something to eat, being the coats didn't cost that much."

"We ever gonna see Daddy again, Lena?"

My heart jumped. I squeezed Dion's shoulder.

"Sure. One day."

Dion looked up at me. "You lying. You said back before we left we wasn't gonna see him no more."

I stopped walking. And since my hand was so tight around Dion's shoulder, she had to stop too.

"You listen to me good, Dion. Our daddy—well, he needs somebody to help him learn to—to treat us right. But he don't know it yet. And when he finds out and gets some help, then maybe we'll see him again."

"What kind of help?" Dion's voice was all tiny.

I started fussing with her collar, trying to figure out what to say next.

"The way he was touching on us, Dion. That don't happen to everybody, you know. Other dads don't do it."

"What touching?" Dion glared at me.

"You know what touching."

She jerked her head so I couldn't fuss with her collar. "He never touched *me*."

I swallowed and took a deep breath. When I first told Marie about my daddy touching me, she said that I was lying, that no father did something like that to their daughter. It took a while for her to believe me. People see what they want to see. I wanted to shake Dion hard now and make her remember. I didn't want her mind shutting off. Not now.

"He *did* touch you, Dion," I said softly. "If you don't re-member then maybe it's best I put you on a bus back home to him."

Dion's bottom lip started quivering. I pulled her close to me and let her cry into my coat. "How come, Lena?" she cried. "How come it has to be us and nobody else? What'd we do bad?"

"We ain't done nothing bad. Not me and you. And it probably ain't only us stuff is happening to. Probably all over the place. It ain't our fault either, you hear me?"

54

"We probably did something bad."

I bit my bottom lip, trying to keep from yelling. "You listen to me good, girlie. Long time ago, I used to think the same thing but I had to sit and think hard about it. Our daddy's a grown-up. Nothing a kid could do to make a grown-up start doing the things he did."

Dion nodded.

"You spend some time thinking hard about it too, Dion. Think about somebody coming to you and you don't want them being there—that's not you doing something bad, okay?"

She nodded again, her lip still quivering.

"If Mama was alive things would be different. But we have to figure out stuff by ourselves and right now I'm figuring it's too cold to be standing out here crying and hungry."

Dion sniffed, then pulled away from me and wiped her eyes. She looked like a tiny little kid in her big peacoat with her eyes all red.

"Was Mama good, Lena?"

I bit my bottom lip again, remembering. "Sometimes I'd come home from school and you and Mama would be in the kitchen making bread. And the sun would be coming through the kitchen window making everything all gold and warm. You'd have flour all up and down your arms and Mama would kind of look at me over your head and smile all proud."

"What would I do?"

"You'd hold up your arms for me to hug you and then I'd hug you and get flour all over me. You thought that was the funniest thing."

I pulled Dion closer to me. "And then later on, we'd sit by the potbelly stove eating bread and jelly and drinking hot chocolate. Maybe that's why you love hot chocolate so much, 'cause of that time."

"Maybe," Dion said. "Where was Daddy?"

I shrugged. "Out. Maybe he was working. Or drinking. I don't remember."

We walked awhile without saying anything. When I was real little, I remember my mama and daddy standing at the bedroom door smiling in at me. He used to have a nice smile. And I remember him asking me whose little girl was I and me saying, "I'm Daddy's little girl." And then he'd tickle me.

"Can I still miss him, Lena?" Dion asked. "Even though?"

"Yeah," I said. "You can miss him."

And we walked on, Dion's missing him outright and my missing him tucked away deep inside, in a long-ago place where I had to think real hard to feel it.

Six

Mama was born in Kentucky. Somewhere near Pine Mountain. I wanted to get us to that mountain, see Mama's home. I didn't know what would happen after that, but maybe those mountains, Mama's mountains, could tell me.

My family wasn't always broke. There was a time when things were all right, when we always had something good to eat and Mama making us those pretty dresses. Before the coal was all gone and before Mama's cancer, we wasn't rich or anything but we got by.

People see somebody poor and they think it's 'cause the person don't want to work or don't have good sense or something, but that's not always true. People all the time looking for a way to blame a person's troubles on the person. In Chauncey, people would look at me and Dion like we was dirt sometimes. Besides the dresses Mama used to make, I don't remember having something new. After she took sick and our daddy wasn't working regular, shirts and pants just sort of showed up at our house, buried deep in the back of a box or wrinkled at the bottom of a bag of clothes. When I started going to Chauncey Middle School where most everybody dressed so nice, I tried to make my clothes look a little better. Got a secondhand iron for two dollars and I'd run it over my stuff and Dion's every morning—figured if the clothes were clean and ironed, they didn't have to be new. People looked anyway. Called us whitetrash. White cockroach. Cracker. There's not a name I haven't heard somebody call me. After a while, the names kind of settle inside you. They start to . . . it's like the names *own* you. I see Dion walking with her head down and I want to yank it up, say, *You can read and you can write and you can walk, girlie, so don't let the names own you.* But she probably wouldn't even know what I was talking about.

"Mama's people were farmers," I said one afternoon. Maybe a week had passed since we'd gotten dropped off in Owensboro. We'd gotten a couple more rides since then and I tried to remember the name of the town we were in. We were sitting out in front of an old shed we'd found the night before. All around us white pine trees shot up tall enough to keep the shed halfway hidden. I leaned back against it. It was pretty out, warm, with the sun shining in splinters through the trees. We were closer to something. I could feel it.

Dion scratched her head and stuck a few pine needles between the pages of her book. She was sitting across from me with her legs folded Indian style. It'd been some time since we'd had a good shower. Dion's hair looked oily. I kept a bottle of water in my bag alongside the toothpaste and brushes and made her brush her teeth every night but her neck looked like it could use a good scrubbing and our nails were chewed and dirty.

She shrugged and looked up at the trees.

"You should know about Mama," I said softly.

"I'd rather just think it was you all along, Lena," she said. "Just you taking care of me." She looked down at her fingernails. "I miss Daddy. I don't want nobody else to miss."

"Knowing about her don't mean you have to miss her, Dion. I just figure it's a way of having a mama."

"You're like my mama, though. You always took care of me. I don't remember her—just shadows and stuff. I miss things I remember—like school, my bed in Chauncey, that pair of red sneakers I left at home." She smiled. It was one of those sad grown-up smiles.

I leaned back against the shed. "Maybe I tell you Mama stories 'cause *I* want to hear them. I don't want to forget her."

"What kind of stuff did her people farm?"

"She never really said . . . or I don't remember. What can you farm up in the mountains?"

Dion squinted and thought for a moment. "Mountain land is sloping and whatnot. Dirt would slide right down it. One good rain and—"

"Well, maybe her people lived in the valley," I said. Sometimes Dion's smartness got on my nerves.

"Well, maybe *you* know what they grew then!" She snapped her book open and started reading again.

I watched her for a few minutes. She was wearing her sweater turned inside out and her blue jeans and hiking boots. Her hair was starting to grow out some and every now and then she wiped it back away from her forehead.

I lifted up my own boots and checked the bottoms for holes. There was a tiny one in the right boot but other than that, they were holding up fine. I leaned back against the shed again and sighed. Some nights, standing out on the road with my thumb out, I got scared. Scared the next ride was going to be our last one—that someone would hurt us real bad or turn us in to the police. But every time we got out of somebody's truck or car, I felt good—

a little bit more free. And times like this, when we could sit and get our minds together a bit, I started getting real sad. I didn't know what was harder—moving or sitting still.

"You know what I miss most about Chauncey, Dion?"

"What?" Dion mumbled, not taking her eyes off her book.

"Remember how on Saturdays we'd go over to Marie's house and take baths?"

Dion nodded. I didn't care that she was only half listening, it felt good to be talking about Marie. Even if I *was* mostly talking to myself.

"Sometimes Marie would come in and sit on the toilet and read—"

"I wish we had a toilet here," Dion mumbled.

"We do. Right in the woods. Go when you gotta go."

She sucked her teeth.

"Anyway, Marie would read this *poet* named—"

Dion looked up. "What poet?"

"This lady named Audre Lorde. She was mostly a poet and sometimes she wrote other things."

Dion went back to her book. "Her poems rhyme? I don't like the rhyming kind."

"Maybe some rhymed and some didn't. I don't know. That's not even the point."

"Well, what's the point then?"

"It's how the words made me feel," I said. Then I started reciting softly—the same way Marie used to read to me. "It went something like 'Living means teaching and surviving and fighting with the most important resource I have, myself . . .'"

Dion closed her book and looked down at the cover.

"'. . . and taking joy in that battle. It means, for me, recognizing the enemy outside and the enemy within . . .'" I stopped reciting, not remembering any more.

"I used to know the whole thing," I said. "Me and Marie memorized it. There was something in it about life and love and work and power that only girls and women got. And something else about a river—the Missisquoi River. She said something about how beautiful it was to fish there and how it was real quiet. . . . That the quiet was sweet and green."

I pulled my knees up to my chin, remembering how peaceful it was in Marie's bathroom, the way the light came in through the windows and turned everything gold. And Marie's soft voice drifting over to me while I played with the tubful of bubbles. It felt like there would always be Saturdays at her house—bubble baths followed by hot chocolate.

"You ever heard of Audre Lorde?"

"No."

I picked the book of maps up and held it close to my face to feel the breeze of the pages. "How far you figure we are from Pine Mountain?"

"It's southeast of here—near Virginia." She exhaled. "Take a look at it instead of fanning yourself with it!"

"Just want to walk the land Mama walked," I said softly.

Dion closed her book. "Bowling Green got a hospital and it's headed in the right direction. We get ourselves there we could head straight east then." She stopped talking and looked at me. "Then we done, Lena? We get to Pine Mountain, we find a place we could stay, go back to school. Huh?"

"Yeah," I said. "In Pine Mountain, we can probably hook up with some of Mama's people. They'll take us in."

Dion smiled. "I'd like that." She came over to the shed and sat down, leaning her head against my shoulder. "I'd like it a whole lot."

Seven

You walk long enough, you get to dreaming about things—the sound of chicken grease popping hot on the stove, the taste of fried chicken when you pull the crispy skin back, the way the steam rises up from the tender meat underneath. And other things too. Like the feel of a nice pillow under your head and sheets when they're fresh out of the wash, smelling like detergent. Windows and doors and hardwood floors underneath your feet.

It was near dark when Dion and me got out to the highway the next evening. We weren't standing on the side of the road two minutes before this Lincoln pulled up and a black woman leaned over asking where we was going. Dion stepped back. We hadn't taken any rides from black people. Not because we didn't want them, just 'cause nobody was offering. Ladies were always a better bet than riding with men but Dion's face scrunched up a bit, the way Daddy's used to when he saw black people. I felt heat rise up to my head and had to put my hand in my pocket to keep from decking her with it.

"Y'all climb on into the back where it's safe," the woman said.

"Get in," I whispered.

Dion looked at me and shook her head.

"Get in that car or I'll leave you standing right here!"

She glared at me a moment, then climbed into the backseat. I climbed in beside her. The woman gave us a strange look, then pulled the car back onto the highway.

"Hi, ma'am," I said. "My name's Lena and that's my sister, Dion." I leaned back against the seat and rolled my window down a bit, hoping me and Dion didn't stink up the car too bad.

"Fine to meet you. I'm Lily."

"Fine to meet you too, Miz Lily."

The woman glanced at me in the rearview and smiled. She had a nice smile. She was old enough to be somebody's grandmother, heavyset with white hair. "Where you girls headed?"

"We live up in Owensboro but our mama just had herself a baby down in Bowling Green. We lost the money she left for bus fare and now we trying to get to the hospital. There was complications so she's going to be there longer than we can be alone. She say come down there."

"How come your mama didn't have her baby closer to home?" Miz Lily asked.

Dion gave me a big elbow in the side. She was pretending to be asleep.

"'Cause of her complications," I said real fast.

Miz Lily nodded. "Well, my daughter, Rona, lives up there near Owensboro—in Thruston. Used to live in Paris."

"France?"

Miz Lily smiled. "She wishes. Paris, Kentucky, girl. You from Owensboro and you don't know Paris, Kentucky?"

I swallowed. "Yes, ma'am, I know it. I just thought maybe you meant Paris, France."

Miz Lily nodded. "Kentucky people like to say *Pay-ris* but not me."

I nodded.

After a moment, she asked, "Where y'all planning on staying tonight?"

I looked at Dion. She opened one eye, then closed it and gave a fake snore.

"Our mama say it's okay to stay in the hospital waiting room. If you drop us off at the hospital, we can—"

"Uh-uh." Miz Lily was shaking her head. "That hospital don't allow children in there after hours. My friend Betty works there. You better call your mama and see if she can make y'all"—she changed lanes before she started talking again—"see if she can make y'all some other arrangements."

"I figure we best not bother her until the morning—being she just had a baby and all."

Miz Lily turned full round and gave us a look. Her driving made me kind of nervous.

"You-all have any people here?"

"No, ma'am."

Miz Lily didn't say anything for a while.

"You say you lost your money back where?"

"Owensboro, ma'am—on our way to the bus, I guess. Fell right out of Dion's pocket."

Dion elbowed me.

"And how'd you get to be in Munfordville?"

"Excuse me?" Somehow I had lost track. We'd had rides, then walked some. I swallowed. I was the one supposed to be keeping track of things. I'd even gotten lazy about writing in the book Marie'd given me. Too busy trying to get me and Dion to the next place.

"How'd you get from Owensboro to Munfordville?"

"We found a ride," I whispered.

"Seems you'd have to be mighty lucky to get this far in one ride. When'd y'all leave?"

"This morning, ma'am."

Miz Lily glanced at me in the rearview.

"I mean . . . we left last night but we stayed with friends . . . up in Elizabethtown."

"So you went across to Elizabethtown then came on down here to Munfordville? That's quite a ways."

"Yes, ma'am." I glanced at Dion and she was looking scared. She shut her eyes again.

"And your people didn't have a couple dollars to give you to take a bus?"

I looked down at my hands. My heart was beating fast and my mind felt like it was racing it. I elbowed Dion but she just went on pretending to sleep.

After a moment, I said, "No, ma'am. They didn't . . . have any."

Miz Lily got quiet again. I breathed in real slow and stared out the window. Poor is poor. My people didn't have any money. I bit my bottom lip. I knew Miz Lily was thinking up a way to get us out of her car. Maybe she knew I was lying. Maybe, even in the dark, she could see it in my eyes. I wanted Pine Mountain to appear out of the darkness like Oz, all full of rainbows and little dancing people.

A truck passed us, lighting the car up. I could see Miz Lily frowning. She looked at me.

"Y'all didn't get scared out on the road?"

"No, ma'am."

"I would think somebody as young as you would get scared . . . being out on the road for the first time."

"It wasn't—I mean, yes, ma'am . . . it got a little scary."

Miz Lily nodded. "I would think so," she said slowly. "How long you say your mama been down in Bowling Green?"

"Since . . . yesterday." I elbowed Dion again. I felt so tired of lying. The lies weren't coming fast enough. Nobody'd asked us this many questions in all our time on the road. I was messing up—stuttering and not remembering what I said two minutes before.

"Yesterday," Miz Lily said. She said it to herself, like she was trying to make herself believe it was true. Then she said it again, real soft. "Yesterday."

"Yes, ma'am."

"You ever heard that saying, 'There's a hundred days in yesterday'?"

I turned back toward the window. "No. But it's real pretty."

"And sad too," Miz Lily said.

We drove awhile with nobody saying anything. I

wanted to pinch Dion, tell her we should make a run for it. But maybe I was imagining Miz Lily knew we was lying and I didn't want to worry Dion over nothing.

"Being I live so close to the hospital," Miz Lily said, "I figure I could put you up for the night, but you need to call, leave word with the hospital about your where-abouts . . ."

I looked down at my hands again and tried not to start bawling. Not from sadness. Just from feeling tired and . . . 'cause the thought of sleeping in a real bed at Miz Lily's house sounded so good. Even if it was just for one night, it was something.

"Mama'd want us to take a bath tonight!" Dion jumped up in her seat. "And eat something hot."

Miz Lily smiled. "I'd want the same thing for my chil-dren. Only I declare I wouldn't have them out all hours of the night trying to get to me. Where's your daddy?"

"Our daddy's dead," Dion said quickly. "Tractor acci-dent got him."

I swear that child can lie when she wants to.

$\mathcal{Y}$ou lie long enough, you start believing your lies. Like the whole time I was fake-dialing the hospital from Miz Lily's living room I was believing, come tomorrow, I was gonna see Mama and her new baby. In the kitchen,

Dion was helping Miz Lily cook and they were talking like old friends about some book Dion had read last summer. I ran my finger along the number in Miz Lily's yellow pages while the hospital phone rang. When a sweet-sounding woman answered, I pressed the receiver down and gave the dial tone a message for Mama. Then I hung up and walked slow around the living room. Miz Lily had one of those neat old-lady houses—the kind with tiny crocheted saucer-looking things laying across the back of her couch and over her table. She had a whole mantelpiece full of pictures—all kinds of pictures, color and black-and-white ones too. I went up to them to get a better look. We never had any pictures in our house— seems Daddy didn't really like looking at them. There's this one Dion carries around with her. It's from when she was a baby. Mama's holding her in her lap and I'm standing between Mama and Daddy. The picture is turning brown around the edges but every now and then I catch Dion taking it out and staring at it. I remember the day we went to have it taken. Mama had wanted it and Daddy hollered the whole morning about how we couldn't afford it. It was the first time I heard Mama say something about dying. She said, *"What if I die? What the children gonna have to remember me by?"* I stared at Miz Lily's pictures, wondering if any of the people in them had passed on. Nobody had ever really explained dying to me—where a person went to after they left this world.

I stood there and looked at Miz Lily's pictures. You stare at someone's pictures long enough, you can make believe the people in them is your own blood family.

When I walked into the kitchen, Miz Lily was rolling out biscuit dough and Dion was putting glasses down on the table. Miz Lily looked at me out of the corner of her eye. "You get a message to your mama?" she asked.

I nodded.

"You tell them to tell her you with Miz Lily Price on Redcliff Road?"

"Yes, ma'am."

Miz Lily started cutting biscuits out with the rim of a glass. Me and Dion watched her, trying not to look too hungry. We hadn't eaten anything since noon and that was only a cold bologna and cheese sandwich we bought at Winn-Dixie. We were trying to hold on to our little bit of money and Dion wouldn't let me steal anything. She said it was too risky.

"I don't have a whole lot to offer but what I got, y'all welcome to. I'm just gonna put these biscuits in the oven and heat up some beef stew I made yesterday." She smiled.

"I never did get used to cooking for one." She slid the pan of biscuits into the oven. A warm blast of air made its way over to me.

I walked over to the oven, trying to get as close as I could to the heat.

"You cold?" Miz Lily asked.

I shook my head, moving my toes around in my boots. I wanted to take them off and let my feet warm up but I didn't want Miz Lily to see my dirty socks.

Dion was pouring milk into the glasses. I tried not to stare at her. I could taste the milk making its way down my throat.

"Bathroom's at the top of the stairs there. Y'all get washed up, I have some cheese and crackers in the refrigerator if you want," Miz Lily said.

I followed Dion up to the bathroom. The tub was long and clawfoot like the one in Marie's house. There was a pink rug on the floor beside it and pink and purple towels piled up on a shelf above it.

"I gotta go," Dion said, dancing around to get her jeans down.

While she went, I stared at myself in the bathroom mirror. My hair was sticking out past my ears now and it was a lighter brown from spending so much time outside. There were tiny wrinkles across my forehead. The rings around my eyes looked darker. I leaned over the sink and splashed warm water on my face. It felt good. Soothing.

Dion flushed and stuck her hands under the running water.

"Wonder if she got bubble bath," she said. She lathered her hands and arms up, then rinsed and held them above the sink.

"What towel do we use?"

I handed her a small blue towel hanging above the bathtub.

"I ain't prejudice, you know," she said, drying her hands and looking at herself in the mirror. "I just ain't used to some things. If we was riding with black people the whole way, I would've just got in that car no question."

"Shouldn't get in *any* car no question," I said. "Should always be careful. But don't be prejudice. Don't be like our daddy."

Dion frowned at herself in the mirror, handed me the towel and bent over to splash water on her face.

"I like Miz Lily," she said, reaching for the towel again without lifting her face up. "She say her husband died on her of a heart attack. Just up and left this world. Ain't that strange?"

"What's so strange about it?"

Dion pulled the towel away from her face and frowned. "The way there's so much dying in the world. You think it's only you but it ain't. It's everybody. Strange. Don't that beef stew smell good?"

She pressed the towel against her face again and held it there a moment. I smiled. When she pulled the towel away, she looked like a little kid.

"I don't want to be prejudice, Lena," she said softly. "I don't want to be like Daddy."

"Good." I tapped her on the back of the head. "We all just people here. Me, you, Miz Lily, Larry, that waitress at Berta's. You keep that in your head, you'll be all right."

Dion nodded. "I get something to eat, I probably be even better."

*W*hen we got back downstairs, Dion tried to take small steps back to the refrigerator to make it seem like she could care less about the cheese and crackers. But I knew by the way her hand was shaking as she reached for everything that she was as hungry and excited as I was.

"How many kids you raised?" I asked, sitting down at the table and slowly making myself a cheese and cracker sandwich. Dion had already stuffed a whole chunk of cheese in her mouth and was following it up with a cracker.

"Oh, I guess about eleven, counting the ones that weren't my own."

"Eleven?" Dion said, spraying cracker crumbs.

Miz Lily checked a pot on the stove, then turned the heat off beneath it. "My own and fosters. I'm sure your mama would do the same thing."

"Do what?" I asked.

"Take in children that needed warm meals," Miz Lily said. "Give them a bed and a safe evening."

Dion nodded but I just sat there staring at her, the cracker going dry in my mouth. I didn't know Mama anymore. Even the memory of her was starting to fade away. And if she was so good, why hadn't she left Daddy when he yelled at her and was mean to us? And why hadn't she found some free or cheap doctor somewhere who could've saved her from the cancer?

"I don't know—"

"Yes she would've!" Dion said, glaring at me. "She would've taken people in."

I shot her a look, hoping Miz Lily hadn't caught what she'd just said.

Miz Lily looked from me to Dion, then bent down to the oven and took the biscuits out.

"If she wasn't in the hospital right now," Dion said quickly, catching herself. "With a new baby and all."

"What'd she have anyway?" Miz Lily asked.

"A little boy," I said. "She named him Jacob."

"That's a fine name. My grandbaby's name is Luther. Prettiest little boy you'd ever like to see." She used a cup to scoop the beef stew into bowls. I watched the steam rise from it.

"Can I have some more milk . . . please, ma'am?" Dion asked.

"Help yourself, child. If it's in that refrigerator, you can have it." Miz Lily finished bringing the bowls of beef stew and the plate of biscuits to the table and sat down.

"Dion," she said. "Since you're the youngest, how about you thanking the Lord for us tonight?"

Dion looked at me, then back at Miz Lily. Dion had her own set of beliefs about God. I shot her a look but she was already opening her mouth to talk.

"God's inside of us," she said, looking a bit frightened.

We had never prayed. Daddy thought it was a waste of time and Mama thought the Lord knew we were thankful, that He could look into our hearts and see it. Ever since she was a real little kid, Dion would talk about God being inside of us rather than up in some heaven somewhere. Once, this woman living next door to us heard Dion say it and told Mama Dion was blaspheming the

Lord's Holy Name. But Mama just smiled and told the woman it was what Dion believed in, so let it be.

Miz Lily looked surprised for a moment. "Well, then I guess your grace will thank the God inside of us, won't it?"

Dion was thoughtful for a moment, then she nodded and we all bowed our heads.

"Thank you, God," she said, talking so low I had to strain to hear her. "For being inside of us and showing us our own way." She stopped for a moment. I lifted my head but Dion and Miz Lily were still bowing theirs so I put mine back down. Steam from the beef stew was rising up, making my mouth water. "Thank you for birds and other peepers keeping us company at night and being inside Miz Lily and me and Lena . . . and all the other people . . . and thank you for food and poetry. Amen."

Miz Lily raised her head and smiled. "That was a fine blessing," she said.

Dion blushed, a tiny smile turning up the corners of her lips. I winked at her, too proud to say anything.

Eight

After dinner, me and Dion did the dishes while Miz Lily sat out on the porch. She kept a small radio propping the outside storm window open above the sink and had music playing—classical music, Dion said, humming along to one of the songs as she dried. The inside window was closed against the cold and I could barely hear the music, but through the window I could see Miz Lily's white head moving slowly like maybe she was humming along too. It looked so nice and peaceful, I made myself a plan to draw it later—Miz Lily's white head with the dim gold light of the kitchen melting over it.

"What are you humming to?" I asked Dion. "You can't even hear that song."

Dion smiled. "I can hear pieces of it and I know the

rest. It's Chopin. We studied him in music class this year." She went back to humming.

I washed the dishes slowly, my mind in a million places at once but mostly it was on Dion. She was too smart to be on the road, needed to be back in school. She could go to college if she wanted. Could be anything she wanted if she set her mind to it.

"What do you want to be when you grow up, Dion?"

She shrugged and continued humming and drying.

"You never think about it?"

She stopped humming. "I guess maybe a college professor like Marie's daddy. Teach poetry. I'd want to teach all kinds of things about poetry." Her eyes lit up suddenly. "Like that music playing. That's poetry without no words in it. And if you was reading a poem, you could read it in the same way."

I frowned. Sometimes it felt bad not to understand Dion—like she was telling me something real obvious and I couldn't get it.

"You could read it like it was—like the words was notes floating on paper. Floating all around the paper." She smiled and went back to humming.

I turned off the water for a moment and strained to hear the music through the glass but I couldn't see words in it. Just music. Music, and places where there wasn't music, then more music. Dion's brain worked different from mine. My brain just saw everything in a straight line but hers moved all around, looked at stuff from different angles.

I turned the water back on so Miz Lily wouldn't hear us. "How come you didn't say nothing when Miz Lily was asking about Owensboro?" I whispered. The question had been riding me the whole night but I hadn't had a chance to ask it.

Dion looked at me. "Because I didn't know the answers," she whispered back.

"You could have thought up something."

She shook her head, picked up a glass and started drying it. "I was too tired to lie some more."

I turned back to the sink and started scrubbing out a pot. I was tired too. Since we'd left Chauncey, we'd met a whole lot of different people and seen a whole lot of places. I knew what the sun looked like now—when it rose up in the morning and right before it set itself down at night. I knew the way the ending day faded the road to blue then black then made it disappear. And the way the cold could come in and turn the whole world winter-brown. I knew too what it felt like to wake up inside of that cold, your clothes damp, your body so frozen it felt like your *bones* was shivering. I closed my eyes a moment.

And on warm days, after a breakfast like the one at Berta's, our bellies full and the sun coming down on our faces as we walked, I knew what it felt like to be free.

I squeezed out the sponge and wiped the counter down. "You could be a professor, you know. You smart enough."

Dion twisted her dish towel into a ball. "It's all dreaming, though. You have to go to school for years and years to teach college."

"It's *not* dreaming!" I whispered. "Other people—they ain't hungry the way you are. I've seen you walk three miles to a library and set there all day reading. Seen you bent over a math sum until later in the night trying to figure out what me and our daddy couldn't even begin explaining to you. So don't tell me it's dreaming."

"You gotta have money to be some college professor, though."

"You get a scholarship—" I stopped, suddenly, remembering something: When I was still living in Chauncey, Marie told me I could be an artist. She said all I needed was a scholarship—get good grades in school and have colleges *begging* to give me money. And now here I was saying the same thing to Dion. "We got to get you back in school."

Dion nodded and hung the towel on the refrigerator handle.

I checked out the window again. Miz Lily was still sitting there, swinging back and forth.

"When our daddy used to come for me," I whispered, turning back to Dion, "I used to wish I was dead. I used to wish the world would just open up and swallow me whole."

Dion's bottom lip started quivering.

"This ain't a sad story so you don't have to cry. All I'm saying is we're free now, Dion. Nobody's holding us back or making us do things we don't want to do. Nobody's making us feel like we ain't worth the water it takes to wash in the morning."

"If we so free, how come we still running and lying then?"

"It won't always be like this, girlie. I got us this far, didn't I?"

"Yeah."

"Well then, I'm gonna get us the rest of the way."

Nine

After we finished the dishes, me and Dion put on our heavy sweaters and went to sit outside with Miz Lily for a while. It was cold but the air felt good with Miz Lily's stew still warming the inside of me. Dion sat down next to Miz Lily on the porch swing and I took a seat on the stairs, turning a bit to face them.

"Night crawlers gone for the winter, I guess," Miz Lily said. "All the rest of the year you can barely hear yourself thinking, the katydids get to talking so loud, the birds just a-singing and frogs croaking. Pretty sounds—all of them, but I like the winter. Can hear my music."

I watched her and Dion moving back and forth. The swing made a whining noise, like it needed oil. But after a while, the sound was soothing, and Dion's eyes started looking heavy. We'd sleep in a bed tonight—with pillows and blankets to pull up over us. We didn't have anything clean to sleep in but it would still feel good—the soft mattress underneath us and windows keeping the cold out. Curtains and doors keeping things private. Dion needed a restful night.

I pulled my knees up to my chin and started thinking. We needed a plan. Something was hammering at the back of my head that I'd been trying not to think about. But the closer we got to Pine Mountain, the harder the thoughts hammered: When I set right down to think about it, Mama's people probably weren't gonna take us in. If they had any interest, they would have come running when Mama died—or at least showed up for the funeral. Chances were, we got to that Pine Mountain, we'd probably be in the same way we were now—except there probably wouldn't be a Miz Lily there, giving us a good meal and such. That night we left Chauncey, getting on the road and just going seemed like the thing to do. But now, all this time passing made stuff more clear. We couldn't go back to our daddy. We couldn't stay on the road forever. Dion needed school—and me, I needed . . . I don't know . . . a home, I guess.

"What you thinking so hard on?" Miz Lily asked quietly.

"Just figuring, ma'am."

Miz Lily frowned. "Child, no need for someone young as you to be looking worried like that. You got years of worry ahead of you. No need to start now. Everything will work out."

"Just hoping Mama and the baby both all right." I bit my lip. Lying to Miz Lily made the stew sit funny in my stomach.

"I don't have to be to work until late morning tomorrow. We'll get up, have ourselves some breakfast and I'll take you right up to the door of that hospital. You'll look rested and fresh when your mama first sets eyes on you."

Dion opened her eyes and yawned.

"Y'all go on upstairs and get ready for bed. Leave your clothes outside the bathroom door. I'll wash them for the morning."

"You don't have to—"

"Better give me the clothes in your bag as well," Miz Lily said, ignoring me. "Your mama probably didn't have the strength to wash before she left."

I nodded and stood. "I really appreciate it, Miz Lily."

Dion got up slowly and stretched.

"And I appreciate your company and y'all doing the dishes," Miz Lily said, waving her hand. "So we're even. Your bedroom is right beside the bathroom. Some of my daughters' old nightgowns are in one of those drawers.

They might be a little worn but they're clean. Now go take your baths and put yourselves to bed. I'll be up in a while."

Dion followed behind me sleepily.

"Lena . . . ," Miz Lily called, when we were almost to the stairs.

I let Dion go on up ahead of me, opened the screen door and stuck my head back out. "Yes, ma'am?"

"Sleep peaceful. Don't go to sleep worrying."

"Yes, ma'am," I said, my eyes filling up. I closed the screen door quickly. I wanted to lay my head on her lap and bawl out everything. I wanted her to hold me—say, *Everything's going to be all right, Lena. Welcome home.*

Ten

Dion had the tub half full by the time I finished getting our dirty clothes together for Miz Lily. The small bathroom was steamy and hot, smelling like lemons. She pointed to the tub filling with bubbles and grinned, then pulled her clothes off and tested the water with her toe. She was getting tall, tall and skinny. It'd been a long while since I'd seen her without clothes on. Her arms and legs had little muscles on them now. Those muscles must've come from all the walking we'd been doing with our knapsacks on our backs.

"You find the shampoo?" I asked, sitting down on the side of the tub.

Dion nodded and climbed in.

She smiled, sinking deep into the water. "The bubble bath smells like real lemons, don't it?"

I nodded. "You wash good. Scrub behind your ears."

Dion turned the water off and sank down further. She sighed.

Downstairs, I could hear Miz Lily padding around. I picked up Dion's clothes and put them in the pile outside.

"You better let her wash your clothes too," Dion said.

I took a towel, then started undressing, my back to Dion. I unrolled the Ace bandage slowly. There were red marks where it ended above and below my breasts. It didn't hurt really, not any more than I figured a bra would.

"Why do you wear that thing anyway?" Dion said.

"You know why. For the truck drivers. Make me look more like a boy."

"You too pretty to be a boy."

I smiled and stepped out of my pants and underwear without answering her, then set the Ace bandage on the toilet-bowl tank, wrapped the towel around me and took my clothes out to the pile.

When I came back in, Dion was sitting up in the tub, scrubbing at her neck with a washcloth.

I kneeled down beside the tub and poured some shampoo into my hand.

"You gonna wash it for me?" Dion asked.

I nodded. "Lean your head back." I took her washcloth, dunked it and squeezed it over her head. Then started lathering. I knew Dion loved it when I washed her hair. It made me feel good to see her, eyes closed and that big smile on her face. Mama used to wash my hair. Her hands always felt real strong.

I heard Miz Lily come upstairs, could hear her sigh as she bent to pick up our pile of clothes, then slowly head down the stairs again.

"Gonna be some kind of ring in this tub after the two of us get finished," I said, squeezing out Dion's hair and watching the gray suds slide down her back into the water.

Dion just nodded and kept on smiling, her eyes shut tight. I dunked the washcloth in the water again, squeezed it out and wiped it over her face. "If you keep your head leant back," I said, "you could open your eyes."

Dion shook her head. "I keep them closed 'cause I'm imagining we're at Marie's house. If I open them, I'll know Marie's house is miles away."

I looked around at Miz Lily's blue walls. Where was the window above Marie's bathtub? Where was the yellow light that came in through it? And Marie. Where was Marie?

Eleven

Mama used to say she wanted to stay at a house long enough to know the workings of it—which floorboards creaked when you stepped on them, what walls shook with a good wind, the sound that same wind made whistling through a crack, the way the spring air smelled coming in an open window. But we never did.

I sat at the top of Miz Lily's stairs thinking long after the house was dark and Dion had climbed into bed. I had had my own bath and the tingle and heat of scrubbing hard was fading from my skin but I wasn't the least bit sleepy.

It had come to me as I sat there scrubbing Dion's head. Me and Dion was like those actors in *The Wizard of Oz*—the thing we'd needed and wanted most was right there inside of us all along. The lion in that movie wanted courage but he really wasn't afraid of nothing. And the tin man, he wanted himself a heart but he had a great big one, right inside of himself. And that funny-looking scarecrow was hankering for a brain—but turned out he was smart as a whip from the start.

Me and Dion—I guess we was kind of like Dorothy—trying to get home, to find ourselves a place. But what came to me as I finished up with Dion's head and sat there watching her give herself one more good scrubbing was that we left the only place that'd ever felt like a home. Chauncey. Not our daddy's house with his ugly ways but Marie and the people who'd been nice to us. Some nights, our next-door neighbor would come over with a whole meal cooked in a pot—stewed beef with rice and greens. At school, my teacher Ms. Cory always asked if things were all right at home and I'd always say "Yeah." Even that man who'd given me and Marie a dollar when we were tap dancing on the street. People in Chauncey had tried to show us they cared in little ways but I was too busy trying to get away from our house to see it.

I had had this dream of Mama's people and Pine Mountain. But all along something else had been kicking in the back of my head. When Mama died, none of her people came to the funeral. Nobody sent us a card or a letter saying they was sorry. Later on, when the authorities came to take us away from our daddy, they tried to get in touch with Mama's people but no one ever responded. Maybe Mama had people out there and maybe she didn't. If she did, those people didn't give two shakes about me and Dion.

And Mama's house. When we first set out, I figured if I could see it, it would give me some answers. But the truth was, I wouldn't know Mama's house if it landed on my head. Probably never really had one even as a little kid. That's why she was always wishing for her own four walls, for a place she could stay awhile. Dion, maybe she still had a dream of Pine Mountain. But the closer I got to Pine Mountain, the more I knew we could go looking all over and probably wouldn't find a single something we could hold close to us and feel good about.

I leaned back against the banister feeling the tears coming on. Outside it was pitch black and the wind sounded soothing—like it would always be coming across the fields here in the wintertime. Miz Lily probably knew those fields better than anyone. She probably knew every creak and whine of this place. That's why she was so peaceful.

After a while, I tiptoed down the stairs into the

kitchen. There was a glowing clock above the refrigerator that said ten-thirty. I picked up the phone and pressed the number, all the while saying a tiny prayer. *Please Lord, give me the courage of that lion . . . And anything else I might need.*

Twelve

Marie's phone rang and rang. It was either Friday or Saturday night, I wasn't sure. Maybe it was too late to be calling anybody. Then Marie's sleepy voice was on the other end.

"Hello, Sherry," she said. "Only your crazy behind would be calling me at this hour."

I swallowed. I'd forgotten about Sherry—the girl who'd been Marie's best friend before I came to Chauncey. I guess they'd gotten to be best friends again. It was stupid of me to think people's lives stopped happening just because somebody walked out of the picture.

"Hello?" Marie said again. Her voice sounded different. I opened my mouth but nothing came out. I could hear my heart beating hard against my chest.

"Lena?" Marie whispered. "Is this . . . is this Lena?"

I nodded, feeling the tears burn up into my eyes and start pouring out. "It's me," I said, my whole face hurting from trying not to cry. "Yeah," I said again. "It's me."

"Oh my god. Where *are* you? Where'd you go? *Are you all right?*"

"Yeah," I whispered. "I mean, yeah, me and Dion doing fine . . ."

"Everybody's looking for you, Lena! My father called all these people. We thought—I was afraid. They were asking me all these questions . . . I thought—" Marie started crying. I wiped my eyes with the back of my hand and held the phone tight against my face.

"We all right, Marie," I said. "Who'd your daddy call? I don't want me and Dion to get separated—"

"Where's Dion? Where are you? I was scared, Lena. My father went to school to talk to Ms. Cory. Everybody's so scared. I thought something terrible happened."

"Dion's here with me. She's real good—sleeping now. Your daddy call cops? Are cops looking for us? Our daddy probably got cops all around looking for us."

Marie was quiet.

"Your father's gone, Lena." She was almost whispering and even in Miz Lily's quiet house, I had to hold the phone real close to hear her. "*We're* looking for you."

"What do you mean he's gone? Where's he gone to?" I felt hot all of a sudden.

"I don't know," Marie said. "They rented your house to somebody else. Every time I walk by it, I wonder about you and Dion. I was so sick with worry. I kept trying to tell myself you two were all right. That you got away from your father." Marie sniffed. "I found that paper you left behind."

"The one with our names?"

"Yeah," Marie said. "It's taped to my mirror. I look at it every day and think about—I miss you!"

Before I left Chauncey I wrote *Elena Cecilia Bright and her sister Edion Kay Bright lived here once* on a piece of paper hoping somebody would find it and think about us. Remember us.

"I'm glad you was the one that found it," I said. *Your father's gone. Your father's gone. Your father's gone.* The words kept repeating themselves in my head. Once, me and my mama went grocery shopping. I was real little but I tried to lift up this big jar of spaghetti sauce anyway. I dropped it and it broke. That's what I felt like now—that broken jar of sauce—busted open.

I sank down against the wall until I was sitting on the floor.

"Lena . . . ," Marie was calling.

"Yeah?"

"I told my father, Lena. I told him everything."

I swallowed. "What'd he say?"

"You mad at me for telling?"

"No, I ain't mad. I just—everybody in Chauncey know?"

"I didn't tell anyone else. Just my father."

"What'd he say?" I asked again.

"He said I should have told him before you left—he called a lot of different places but people kept telling him he had to be related to you and Dion if he wanted some information. He was going to make believe he was your father but I told him you and Dion weren't supposed to be living with your father. He was real upset about it. I think he feels bad that he wasn't nicer to you and Dion. He said the social service people keep telling him that all they could do is put a search out for you. And when they found you, they'd—"

"They'd separate us," I said. "Just like they did the last time."

"They said they'd try to find a home for you and Dion. My daddy calls them every day—to see if anyone's found you two. Where *are* you, Lena?"

Your father's gone. Out of our lives—forever and ever

amen. Me and Dion's leaving hadn't made him worry and search all over for us. It'd made him free to move on. Maybe I'd never believed a hundred percent that it was just me and Dion left of our family. But I believed it now. I used to say that blood didn't mean anything but now I was thinking that blood *did* mean something. My daddy was real messed up but he was all we had. And now we didn't even have that raggedy thing.

"My daddy really gone, Marie?" I whispered.

"Yeah. People at the agency told my father they put a search out for him too but no sign yet."

"People disappear all the time. You hear from your mama?"

"No."

"Maybe she's somewhere with my daddy."

Marie laughed, then sniffed again. "Lena, I thought . . . I was scared. I read the newspaper every day looking for signs of you and Dion."

"It rained sometimes," I said. "Those nights it was real cold and felt like we could never get dry. I don't ever want to sleep outside in the rain again." *Your father's gone.* I felt like I could just go on and on—talk right into the morning. Tell everything. "We was scared that first night but we got a ride from a nice lady and it felt like everything was going to be all right then."

"Lena, tell me where you are. My father and I could come—"

"In Kentucky. This other nice lady—not the one from Ohio—let us stay at her house tonight."

"What about tomorrow? Where will you be tomorrow?" Marie sounded desperate, the way she sounded the night me and Dion left.

"I don't know about tomorrow."

"Don't leave again. Don't go somewhere I can't find you!" Marie sniffed.

"We're okay, Marie. For real we are."

"You coming back?" Marie whispered. "What about school and being an artist?"

"No place to come back to, Marie."

"You can come *here*, Lena. To *my* house."

I closed my eyes and tried to imagine me and Dion living in Marie's big house with her daddy. Tried to imagine us all waking up together and getting ready for school. Imagining it made me smile but I knew it could never happen, not with her daddy not really liking white people and them being so rich and all. Two white girls like me and Dion weren't gonna fit in that house.

"I could ask him . . . ," Marie was saying. "Soon as he gets home from his stupid date. At least let me ask, Lena. He's different now. Now that I told him everything—it's like . . . I think he knew there was no way he could keep my mother from leaving but there was a way he could have kept you and Dion from going. That changed him. He really wants to find you and Dion. He told me he wants everything to turn out all right."

I swallowed. Outside, I could hear an owl *whoo-whoo*ing.

"You ask him," I said, feeling real tired now. All I wanted was to climb in bed beside Dion, to sleep peaceful one night before we got back on the road.

"Give me the number there."

I got up and recited the number off Miz Lily's phone, not caring anymore about the lies we had told Miz Lily. It didn't matter what anybody knew about us anymore. It was only me and Dion in the world now.

"Promise you won't leave there!"

"I won't."

"Promise me!"

"I promise."

"I'll call you real early in the morning," Marie said. "You stay near the phone, okay?"

"Okay," I said, feeling a little bad for Marie. She still had a lot of hope and faith. We was real different that way.

"And Lena?"

"Yeah."

"Lena, I'm glad you and Dion are all right."

I smiled. When I was still living in Chauncey, I used to always tell Marie how I wanted to do like this singer Jimi Hendrix and kiss the sky. Having Marie say she was glad I was all right was like kissing the sky. Knowing there was this person out there feeling glad about us being okay.

"Yeah," I whispered. "Me too."

Thirteen

I woke up early to the smell of bacon frying. Dion was still sound asleep beside me, her hair sticking up all over her head. I climbed out of bed and made my way to the bathroom. Miz Lily had left our clothes outside the bedroom door. They were folded real nice. I found my jeans and T-shirt and then took my flannel shirt from the bottom of the pile and went into the bathroom, all the while trying not to think about Marie calling.

I stood under the shower water a long time, not sure when I'd be able to take another. It felt warm against my back and I let it run over me a little while longer before soaping up and washing my hair again. Figure between the night before and this morning, I'd have one of the cleanest heads in Kentucky.

When I came out of the shower, Dion was sitting on the toilet all sleepy-eyed.

"I'm gonna take me another bath." Her voice was hoarse.

"Well, take it in a hurry. Miz Lily already got breakfast started." I finished drying off and started wrapping my band around my chest.

Dion watched me without saying anything.

"We getting in another truck today?" She poured some bubble bath in the tub and started the water running. Her hair was kind of sticking up all over her head from her going to bed with it wet and I guess, until I got into that shower, mine hadn't looked much better.

I shrugged, finished pulling my clothes on and kind of finger-combed my hair in the mirror. Dion climbed into the tub and started washing herself right away.

"It was nice sleeping in a real bed."

"Yeah, it was," I said. "I'll bring you in some clean clothes. Make sure you fill yourself up good at breakfast."

Dion nodded without looking at me.

*M*iz Lily was on the phone when I came downstairs. I stood there waiting to take it from her.

"I have to go," she said quickly. "You just keep an eye out, you hear? I'll talk to you soon."

When she hung up, she looked at me and smiled. "You expecting a call, sugar?"

I shook my head, feeling the grin leaving. "No, ma'am. I don't know what I was thinking."

Miz Lily nodded. "You sleep all right?"

"Yes, ma'am. I slept just fine."

She had set the table real pretty with a jarful of yellow flowers in the center and these nice sky-blue plates and mugs set down on top of a flowered tablecloth. There was a big pile of bacon beside the flowers and a stack of biscuits next to the bacon. The clock above the refrigerator said eight-fifteen. I looked at the phone, then turned and bumped eyes with Miz Lily.

A few minutes later, Dion came downstairs, her hair still wet. She pressed the arm of her shirt to her nose, took a deep smell and smiled. "Thanks for washing our stuff, Miz Lily."

"You sleep good, Dion?" Miz Lily asked, bringing a bowl of scrambled eggs over to the table.

"Yes, ma'am."

"Can I help you with anything, Miz Lily?" I asked, trying to keep my mind away from the phone.

She shook her head. "Y'all just get to eating."

She was wearing an apron. Underneath it, she had on a dark dress with a string of pearls hanging around her neck and nice shoes that matched the dress. Her hair was curled up all over her head.

"Your hair looks real nice," I said.

Miz Lily shook her head and laughed. "Hush, girl. I just throw a few curlers in it at night and see what the morningtime brings."

She brought a container of orange juice to the table and filled up three glasses. "Y'all must be so excited about seeing your mama." She stood there waiting for an answer.

Dion was sitting chewing on a piece of bacon. She kind of looked at me, then nodded. Seemed like forever ago we'd been in Miz Lily's car telling her about going to see Mama.

"Yes, ma'am." I put a biscuit and some eggs on my plate.

"You say you talked to her last night?"

I swallowed. Had I said I talked to her?

"No, ma'am," Dion said real fast. "Lena say she talked to the nurse."

"And the nurse told her you was coming today?"

Me and Dion nodded.

"You don't by chance know that nurse's name, do you?"

"No, ma'am."

"You say your mama's last name is . . . ?"

"We didn't say," Dion said.

Miz Lily smiled. "Well, my goodness. I'm sitting here in my house with strangers don't even know their last name."

"Bright," I said. "Lena and Dion Bright."

Dion glared at me but didn't say anything.

"Pretty names." Miz Lily went back to the stove. I looked at Dion and shrugged. I wanted to holler it—say, *What's the use of lying about anything anymore? Our daddy's gone. Get used to it.*

"Hope y'all like grits 'cause I made a pot of them." She wrapped a dish towel around the handle, then brought the pot over to us. I'd only had grits a couple of times and couldn't remember them.

Dion tried not to squish up her face as Miz Lily put two big spoonfuls on her plate, then two more on mine.

I took a tiny bite. The grits tasted like paste with little bits of sand in it.

"Uh-uh," Miz Lily said, frowning at me. "Put some butter and salt on them. Stir it all up. That's what makes grits taste like anything." She smiled, put the pot back on the stove and brought a cup of coffee with her over to the table. "Grits are just an excuse to fill up on butter and salt."

I sprinkled some salt on them, then put a pat of butter on top. It looked pretty with the yellow melting into the white. Dion did the same thing.

"Now stir it all up," Miz Lily said.

We stirred the grits and each took a small bite.

"Hey, these taste good," Dion said.

Miz Lily smiled. I took another bite, liking the feel of the little grains in my mouth.

Miz Lily picked up a piece of toast and put a forkful of egg on it. "They taste good when you mix them with some egg and toast too."

Dion did like Miz Lily, taking some toast and egg in her mouth then a bite of grits and chewing the whole thing together.

"I bet I could eat this every day," she said.

"Me too," I said, really meaning it.

The phone rang and I nearly jumped right out of my seat. Miz Lily gave me a strange look as she got up to answer it.

"Lena don't care much for loud sounds," Dion said quickly.

Miz Lily nodded, still looking at me. I tried to keep my eyes down on my plate.

"Rona," Miz Lily said. "How you doing, sugar? And how's that grandbaby of mine?"

Fourteen

Miz Lily drove us right on up to the entranceway of Bowling Green General. The hospital seemed bigger than a lot of the other ones me and Dion had stopped at and even though it was early, there was lots of people going in and out.

Dion was sitting up front with Miz Lily. When the car stopped, Dion turned to me. She looked sadder than I'd seen her in a long time.

"Really appreciate everything," I said, looking away from Dion.

"If I wasn't running late, I'd come in with y'all, make sure you get to your mama—"

"No, you don't have to," I said real quick.

"Well, let me climb out and give you girls a hug."

We all climbed out of the car. Me and Dion lifted our

knapsacks on our backs. It was real pretty out, blue and warm. Miz Lily hugged us both real hard and told us to take care of ourselves.

"Let me write down my number in case anything goes wrong," she said. She took a small pad and a pen out of her purse and wrote her number down real quick.

I looked around for a phone figuring I'd call Marie one more time after Miz Lily left, tell her we were gone. That we were on our way someplace else now.

Miz Lily finished writing her number and folded some money into it. Seemed people were always handing us money. Keep it up, reckon we'd be rich soon.

I took the money without objecting. We all three hugged again and then Miz Lily's car was pulling away. Me and Dion watched it a moment, then headed into the waiting room.

There were white chairs lined up in rows and a desk with a couple of people working behind it. We took a seat in the back of the waiting room and Dion took out her book of maps and opened it up to Kentucky.

"Figure we head east real early," she said. "Get to Pine Mountain with lots of daylight left. We could start looking for some of Mama's people before it gets dark. Maybe get us a nice bed to sleep in again . . ."

I stared out the window, trying to concentrate on what Dion was saying. Her voice sounded far away, like it was some stranger talking to me from underwater.

"Hey, girlie . . . ," I said slowly. "I talked to Marie last night."

Dion looked up at me and stopped talking. "She say anything about our daddy?"

I nodded. "Say he left Chauncey."

Dion closed the book of maps and folded her hands over them. She looked slowly around the waiting room. "Where'd he go?"

I shrugged. "She doesn't know. Say he left a while ago. The way I figure, he probably ain't coming back."

Dion's chin trembled but she didn't say anything.

"Marie say she was gonna talk to her daddy see if we could come live with them but she ain't called back. I'm gonna try her again, though."

"Her daddy ain't gonna want us," Dion said. She wiped at her eyes and tried to sit up straighter. I looked around the waiting room and saw a black lady sitting at the guard desk watching us. When she saw me looking, she looked away.

"I been thinking since this morning about something. Maybe the social worker people ain't so bad," I said.

"Maybe we turn ourselves in we could get us a nice place to live, like with somebody like Miz Lily."

"Ain't going to no social worker people," Dion whispered, her voice fierce. When she looked at me, her eyes were narrow as slits and her cheeks were burning red.

"Where you going then, girlie?" I asked. I wasn't mad at her for getting mad. Just tired. Tired of everything.

"Mama's people!"

I put my hand over Dion's. On the cover of the map book there was a picture of the globe, looking all blue and green and promising.

"Mama's people ain't gonna take us in, Dion. I don't even know where to start searching when we get to Pine Mountain."

"We start with the *phone* book," Dion said. "Look under her maiden name—Charles."

"And we find out everybody in that phone book's name is Charles. And then we find the Charles relatives that didn't even come to her funeral or come get us the *first* time the social work people took us away."

Dion's chin trembled again. After a moment, a tear slipped out of her eye. She snatched one of her hands from underneath mine and wiped it away, real quick without taking her angry eyes off me.

I looked over at the lady but she wasn't watching us no more.

"I ain't going to no social worker people, Lena Bright. You go, then you go by your own damn self!"

I didn't say anything. It'd been a long time since I heard her curse and it sounded loud in the quiet waiting room. Loud and painful as a punch.

"I'm gonna go try Marie again."

Dion nodded and opened the map book again. I walked up to the guard desk.

"Excuse me, ma'am. Can you tell me where's the phone?"

The woman smiled at me and got up. "I'll show you," she said, and walked me two feet down the hall, then went back over to her desk and stood there, looking back and forth between me and Dion.

I got the operator and made a collect call to Marie's number. It was busy. I smiled. That was a good sign. Maybe she was talking to her daddy about us. Maybe things were happening. I hung up and walked back over to Dion.

"I'm gonna try again in a while," I said. "It was busy."

When I tried a few minutes later, the phone rang and rang. My hands was trembling when I walked back over to Dion.

We sat there just sort of looking at each other and looking away. I kept my hand on top of the hand Dion still had on the book. Announcements came over the loudspeaker, people came in and out. All around us the world seemed to be going on about its business.

Fifteen

I wish I could say I was surprised to see Miz Lily walking into that waiting room, walking fast toward us with that beautiful head of white curls. My mama used to always say you can't stop hoping. Even when everything else in the world seemed to be gone, she said that's the thing you got to hold on to. Hope.

Me and Dion watched Miz Lily coming fast toward us without moving save for Dion slipping that book of maps back into her bag.

"I declare," Miz Lily said, shaking her head. "I *knew* something wasn't right about all this. I thought I raised enough kids like y'all to know the signs. But I must be losing my touch."

"Our mama's resting—" Dion began.

Miz Lily held up her hand. "Y'all don't have to lie any-more. Nobody sitting in this immediate area is gonna hurt you. That there's my friend Betty I told you worked here. She's been keeping an eye on y'all." Miz Lily waved and the woman sitting at the guard desk waved back and nod-ded. Miz Lily sat down beside us and put her hand on Dion's shoulder.

Dion looked down at her hands and didn't say any-thing.

"Y'all don't have a mama, do you?" she asked softly.

I shook my head, feeling myself getting teary again.

"I figured that when Dion didn't mention her in her prayers. And what about your daddy? Is he living?"

"Yeah," I said hoarsely. "But we don't know where he is. Last he was in Ohio but he ain't no more."

"And this Marie child I talked to—"

I jumped. "Marie called?"

Dion lifted her head, looking wildly from Miz Lily to me, then back again.

Miz Lily nodded. "Said her father wants y'all to stay with them."

I pressed my hand against my leg and pinched, hard. I didn't want to be dreaming, didn't want to find myself awake somewhere without this happening. Dion looked down at her hands again but she was grinning, grinning wide.

"My precious Lord," Miz Lily said under her breath. "To think you thought I believed your mama was here. I wasn't gonna let you out of my sight until I had some sure facts. I couldn't get them with you two hanging around so I asked Betty to keep an eye on you until I had my answers. I wasn't going to call the police until I checked everything else out. I *knew* something wasn't right. Then just as I was about to pick up the phone to call another social service agency, it rang."

"We're sorry, Miz Lily," Dion said. "We don't care much for lying, and you being so nice to us and all."

Miz Lily looked down at Dion, her face melting. She took Dion's chin in her hand and stared at her a moment without saying anything. Then she looked over at me and shook her head. "But y'all are just *babies*."

Me and Dion didn't say anything.

"Called the four Brights listed around here and none of them knew of y'all so I figured you didn't have people around here. Called a few agencies and nobody seems to have a record of you. It's like y'all are *spirits*. Just appeared."

Dion shook her head. "No, ma'am. We real."

Miz Lily smiled and ran her hand over Dion's head. "You sure are, child. . . . Well, come on. I want to go home and call Marie's father and get this thing straightened out."

She went over to speak to Betty, then came back over to us.

Me and Dion got up and walked in a line behind her right out of that hospital. When we got to the door, Dion turned and looked at me, a big grin eating up her face.

Sixteen

Miz Lily and Marie's daddy talked for more than an hour while me and Dion sat in the living room, leaning forward so that we could hear as much as possible. Seemed Marie's dad was explaining about Chauncey, about me and Dion too but mostly about the town and such. Miz Lily kept going, "Oh, Lord" and "Oh my" and "A professor, huh? Well, ain't you something."

There was a lot of talk about social work agencies and how Marie's dad was gonna handle the paperwork and all. Seemed he'd met a bunch of people working in foster care right there in Chauncey. I could hear Miz Lily explaining to him about red tape and them having to contact next of kin and such. "But looks like there's really no next of kin to worry about. Seems these girls really on their own, don't it?" she said, her voice dropping down to a whisper.

Marie's dad must have been going on and on because Miz Lily had gotten real quiet.

"I guess this is it, huh, girlie?"

Dion looked at me and smiled. "I guess so."

Neither of us wanted to say it right out loud. Didn't want to jinx it.

"Well," Miz Lily said. "If you wasn't taking them in, I sure would. They're good girls, sweet and polite as they could be. But you're right—get them back to what's familiar and back to their old school. No doubt they'll catch right up."

Me and Dion looked at each other again and grinned.

I could hear them talking over a plane schedule. I bit my lip, trying to hold back my excitement, but Dion was grinning. We had never been on a plane before. Rich people took planes. I felt rich inside, like everything about the world was falling in place and there wasn't so much empty inside of me anymore. I grabbed Dion's hand and squeezed it.

"We going on a plane, Lena," she whispered.

"Yeah, girlie. Me and you way up in the air."

Dion bounced herself against the back of the sofa. "A plane," she whispered again. "Me and you up in the air."

"What's the first thing you gonna do when you get . . . get to Chauncey, Lena?"

I smiled. "I'm gonna hug Marie and then I'm gonna touch all the walls in her house. And then I'm gonna send Larry back his money and tell him we all right."

"I'm gonna buy some bubble bath," Dion said. "And tomorrow morning I'm gonna eat a ham and cheese sandwich for breakfast!"

It was a two-hour flight back to Columbus where Marie and her dad would pick us up and drive us the hour and a half back to Chauncey. There wasn't any airport in Bowling Green. Miz Lily would drive us to Nashville and put us on a plane there, she said, and we'd be back to Chauncey by dinnertime. I felt my heart lift up in my chest. The sun was shining through the living room window, making a bright patch on the hardwood floor. I felt like that patch of sun—all bright and warm.

Dinnertime, I kept thinking. *Home by dinnertime.*

Seventeen

It was near eleven o'clock when Miz Lily got to fixing us some sandwiches and packing up some store-bought cake for us to take. Me and Dion helped, putting food in bags and washing up the breakfast dishes we'd left in the sink that morning. After a few minutes, I had to go upstairs to the bathroom, sit down on the toilet and let myself cry. It was almost over. There wasn't nothing to be afraid of anymore. Marie's daddy wasn't going to let anything happen to me and Dion, and my own daddy was gone. When I tried to get a picture of his face, it was all blurry and far away. Dion would be the one to remember it, to remember the good things about him—the way I was the one to remember them about Mama.

When I came back downstairs, Miz Lily was still getting us ready for the trip and talking about Marie's dad.

"He's a good man. I can tell by talking to him. All he's been through trying to find y'all. But if you girls don't like it, you know you can always come back to my house," she said, her eyes getting all soft.

I tried to remember what I could about Marie's dad. He had never said much to me but he always let us come over on Saturdays to take baths and drink hot chocolate. When he saw Marie and me was getting to be friends, he left us alone. He loved Marie more than anything.

"Marie told me he was looking all over for us," I said.

Miz Lily nodded. "He said he was worried sick—the idea of you two somewhere on the road. Said he wasn't going to stop looking until he found you, made sure you were safe. Made sure you had a home."

I smiled and looked away from her—my throat getting tight. He had been worrying about *us*. Worried sick. That meant something. *Made sure you had a home.* He had said that. Once, Marie told me she caught her daddy sitting in the dark crying. He was staring at a picture of her mother. When she turned on the lights, he wiped his eyes real quick and looked away. Another time she said she had asked him about not liking white people and he said it was 'cause white people didn't like blacks. He'd said none of it's right, though. I bit my lip remembering something else—that one time Marie had said me and her daddy were

128

alike 'cause we wanted people to just be able to be people. To just be able to live. And now here he was, making sure me and Dion had a home. A safe place *to live*.

"I'm going to keep in touch," Miz Lily was saying. "And you write and tell me how you are. I stuck a card with my address in each of your knapsacks. If you lose it, I'm listed. Lily Price."

Dion went over to where she was standing by the counter and hugged her, her hands still dripping with dishwater.

"You're good," Dion whispered.

Miz Lily smiled. "We all got our skeletons, honey. Next person walking down the street might not think I'm as good as you do. My daughter could probably tell you a hundred stories about why I wasn't a good mother. I've done my share of right and wrong."

"You're good to us," I said.

"Then that's what matters, isn't it?"

Me and Dion nodded.

"Oh my stars," she said when they pulled away from each other. "Let me go get my camera."

She climbed upstairs slowly, then came back down a little while later with a Polaroid and made me and Dion stand out on the porch. We stood with our arms around each other's shoulders smiling into the bright sunlight.

"I'm gonna buy a nice frame when I leave work tomorrow and put it right up there on the mantelpiece with my other pictures."

$\mathcal{W}$e didn't talk much on the drive to the airport. Dion could barely sit still and I had to bite my lip to stop imagining that plane going up into the air.

But I was thinking about Chauncey too. Seemed my mind was racing my body to get there. I'd never spent the night at Marie's house but I still knew every nook and cranny of that place. Some Saturdays we'd just go from room to room, Marie telling me everything she could remember happening there. I'd touch photos and bedspreads and paintings and try to imagine living in a place where I knew the history of it the way Marie did. Now I would be living there with Marie. I closed my eyes for a moment, trying to imagine it. I was already seeing Marie's grinning face at the airport, her and her daddy standing there. I smiled. It seemed impossible that come Monday, I'd be sitting in Ms. Cory's history class again. I was gonna work real hard this time. Maybe Marie was right. Maybe I could go to college if I wanted.

Dion took my hand. When I looked over at her, she was smiling. I squeezed her hand real hard, then leaned back against the seat and stared out at Kentucky.

Eighteen

When we climbed out of the car, Miz Lily looked kind of teary-eyed and so did Dion. We walked to the airport all hugged up, Miz Lily's arm soft and warm against my shoulder.

Dion would probably be writing her every other day or so. Dion get attached to a person, she holds on.

"Y'all know to call me the minute you step off that plane, right?"

"Planes scary, Miz Lily?" Dion asked. We were getting close to the ticket place and she started walking slower.

"Shoot, no." Miz Lily smiled. "About the most exciting ride there is."

I wrapped my arm tighter around Miz Lily's waist. Maybe she'd never been in a car going ninety down a dark highway or sitting high up in a truck trying to take a narrow turn. Me and Dion had. We'd seen the inside of more vehicles than we'd ever want to again. Maybe a plane *was* exciting but I was ready for all my riding to end.

Miz Lily had made special arrangements with the stewardess ladies on the plane. We were to sit right up front where they could keep a watch on us and Marie's dad was going to have to show identification before we could leave with him.

There weren't many people waiting for the plane. I tried to give Miz Lily the money she'd given us that morning but she shook her head. "You hold on to that. Buy you and Dion something nice when y'all get back to Chauncey." She hugged me and Dion again, handed us our tickets and walked with us into the plane. Dion walked carefully, touching the backs of the seats and looking all around her. The stewardess lady was standing right up front. She smiled at us, then talked to Miz Lily while me and Dion put our knapsacks under the seats in front of us and sat down.

"You-all call me when you get to the airport, you hear?" Miz Lily said. "Make sure you call me the minute you get there."

Me and Dion nodded. Miz Lily gave us another kiss.

"Miz Lily," I said. "I really appreciate everything—"

"Hush, child." She waved her hand at me and smiled. "I should be thanking y'all for giving me some time away from that job of mine. Put your seat belts on."

We buckled our seat belts while she stood watching us. Dion threw her a kiss. Miz Lily made as if to catch it and put it in her purse, then headed slowly down the aisle. I watched her make her way out of the plane, my eyes filling up.

"You think we'll ever see Miz Lily again, Lena?" Dion asked. She reached up over her head and turned the light off and on a couple of times, then put her hands on her lap and looked at me.

Seemed like someone was always leaving someone, like that's the way the world worked—people were born and people died, people left and people came. It was like the world was saying you can't have everything you want at the same time.

"I reckon we'll see her again," I said. "And you know something, girlie? Even if we don't, we had a chance to make a good friend."

"And to eat some grits!" Dion said.

I laughed.

Dion frowned, thinking. "It's okay to miss her, huh? And to talk about her from time to time?"

When I nodded, Dion smiled, then took out her book of poetry and started reading. She'd be all right, that Dion would. And me? Maybe I'd be all right too.

Outside, the sun was hanging pretty over some mountains in the distance. I watched the pink and gold light spread itself over the green for a while, making a promise to myself to write about it one day. All of it. The stuff I'd written down in the book Marie gave me and the stuff I'd left out too. I wanted to remember it. And I wanted Dion to remember too. Mama told me once that if you remember all the places you been in your life, you'll have a better sense of where you're going. I pressed my shoulder against Dion's and smiled. I had a real good sense of where we were going.

After a while, I took the sandwiches out of one of the brown paper sacks, folded the wrinkles out of the bag and started sketching. I wanted to catch the glow of the sun, catch the way the mountains moved their faces up toward it.

When the plane started to take off, Dion put her book down and took my hand. We looked at each other and started laughing, surprised at how fast the plane was moving. The noise it made was louder than anything I'd ever heard.

"Look out the window," I said. Dion pressed her face against it and smiled as the plane lifted up into the air.

A woman sitting across from us leaned over and asked where we were going. I looked at Dion then back at the woman again. "Me and my sister," I said, feeling a grin spread wide across my face, "we heading home."

Then Dion grinned, pressed her face against the window again and started humming.

And me, I sketched that mountain kissing that sky.